THE HYBRIDS

MARISA CHENERY

ISBN-13: 978-1-98865-936-7
Cover Art By: Ammonia Book Covers
Cover Model: Jason Aaron Baca

CONTENTS

HER ANCIENT HYBRID

Brolach is old. Ancient. A hybrid, half vampire and half werewolf, he's a true immortal who can never die. He's lived for three thousand years but has slept buried for two of them. It isn't until a female comes to the hill where he sleeps that he comes awake, ready to protect her, his vampire side knowing she's his mate.

Physically threatened by her ex-boyfriend while out on a hike in the grasslands has unexpected results for Waverly. A man, muddy and covered in dirt, explodes out of the ground to rescue her. After the initial shock of learning that he is both vampire and wolf, she finds herself more than willing to bring him into her life, especially when he turns his attention on her.

With the help of Waverly, Brolach begins to adjust to the world he's awakened to. But the new life he sets about making with his mate is soon threatened by a danger from the past—the same one that had killed his family and buried him alive two centuries before.

CHAPTER ONE

Waverly shrugged her backpack higher onto her shoulders as she walked through a section of the grasslands in the Grand River National Grassland in South Dakota. She lived in Lemmon, which was a smallish town of over a thousand people and was close to where she now hiked.

It was a gorgeous Saturday in June. Waverly tried to come out to the grasslands as much as she could and spend the day hiking. The area boasted rolling hills, river breaks, and scattered badlands. It was mostly made up of mixed grass prairies.

While with her ex-boyfriend, she hadn't had as many opportunities to enjoy this particular pastime. James hadn't been a hiker and had taken exception to her going off on her own to the grasslands. He really hadn't liked her to do much without him, which was part of the reason she'd broken up with him a few months before. He hadn't taken it well, but it'd been time for her to move on.

Waverly had just topped a hill when the sound of her name being called reached her. She turned and couldn't believe who she saw running toward her. It was James, the last person she wanted to see. Lately, he'd been calling her, almost begging her to take him back. She hadn't been impressed.

After he finally met up with her and had caught his breath, Waverly asked, "What are you doing here, James? Did you follow me?"

He gave her a smile. "Maybe a little. I'd come by your place and saw you driving away so I decided to see where you were going. When I realized you were coming here, I sat in the parking lot for a bit, not sure if I wanted to take the hike as well."

"I see you did in the end. What do you want?"

"You. As my girlfriend."

She blew out a breath. "We've been over this on the phone several times. I don't want to get back together. You were starting to suffocate me. You wanted to control my life."

"What if I promise I'll stop?"

"That won't change my mind."

"Why not? I love you. We're meant to be together."

Out of the six months they'd been a couple, not once had either one of them said the big "L" word. Waverly doubted James actually felt that strongly about her. Obsessed maybe, but definitely not love.

She shook her head. "No, you don't. You're just thinking that way because we broke up. You want to use it as another tactic to get me back."

"You're wrong. I've always loved you since our first date and never told you."

Would James ever give up? He had to know she wanted to keep things the way they were between them. She'd only said so at least a dozen times. Being apart from him showed Waverly she hadn't made a mistake. He wasn't the right guy for her and really hadn't been from the start of their relationship.

"Forget it, James. What's done is done. You have to get past it and move on with your life."

His smile slowly died. In its place a sneer formed. "I won't let you walk away. You're mine."

"No, I'm not."

"If I say you are, then you are."

James' words came out in anger. Rage was written all over his face and in the stiff lines of his body. Waverly had never seen him like that before. He reached for her arm and roughly jerked her closer.

He brought her nose to nose with him and bellowed, "You'll either stay with me or I'll make you regret it." James cruelly dug his fingers into her biceps.

That was when Waverly grew scared. James wasn't a big man, by any means, but he had three inches on her five-foot-seven and weighed at least twenty pounds more than she did. She struggled to break his grasp, which had no effect on him. He shook her like a rag doll.

Even though there wasn't anyone around, and couldn't be for miles, Waverly screamed as her fear tried to take her over. She really hadn't known the man she'd called boyfriend and had slept with. It was as if he had two personalities, and she was getting her first introduction to his crazy side.

James raised his free hand and balled it into a fist. Waverly lifted her arm to ward off the inevitable blow that was about to come. He was going to hit her, and there was nothing she could do to stop him.

Just as his fist headed toward her, there was a giant explosion of earth a few feet beside them. James froze and then turned his head to look in that direction as she did. Waverly's breath caught in her lungs. There was a man covered in mud and dirt standing next to the large hole. He snarled his upper lip, showing a fang, and let loose with an animalistic growl that would have done a wolf proud. It was his eyes that had her unable to breathe. The

4

jade-green orbs glowed as his gaze latched on to her ex.

* * * *

Brolach was three thousand years old and had "slept" through two thousand of them. He was the only one of his kind—a hybrid, half vampire and half werewolf. Even though he'd been under the ground for so long, he'd been partly aware of the surface world. People traversed the area, and as the years went by, the language they spoke changed. His mostly asleep brain learned it enough to understand it.

Something brought his mind closer to wakefulness before he was ready to be roused. There was a presence on the hill where he was buried. It drew him and captured his attention as nothing had done for centuries. It was female, which caused a part of him to stir.

Soon a male joined her. Brolach listened to their conversation, his sensitive hearing able to pick up each word spoken. The longer he listened, the more he awakened from his long slumber. The need to protect the female came to life. Never before had he felt like that toward a member of the opposite sex. The vampire side of him instinctively knew she was his. His mate. The werewolf wouldn't know for sure until he had her scent in his nose.

The sound of the male's voice raised in anger would have had Brolach's hackles rising if he'd been in wolf form. It wasn't until the female screamed that he came fully awake. The sound was full of fear.

Brolach burst out of the ground. His fangs lengthened at the sight of the male holding the female by the arm with a raised fist, ready to strike. He snarled his upper lip and growled a warning. All his protective instincts roared to the surface. He latched his gaze on to the human who threatened his mate.

He surged into action. Brolach closed the distance between them, broke the male's grip on the female, and tossed him away. He landed with a shriek and then whimpered as Brolach approached him. He was tempted to kill the weaker male, to drain him of the blood he needed after his long sleep, but he decided against it. This new world he awoke to wasn't the same as the one he'd known. Death wasn't doled out so easily or frequently as it'd once been.

Rather than take the male's life, Brolach reached for the werewolf half of himself and brought on the change. He took on his wolf form in a matter of seconds. His hackles rose, and he growled as he made a threatening step toward the male. That was enough to send the human scuttling backward before he clumsily gained his feet and took off running down the hill.

Once he was sure the male wouldn't come back, Brolach turned to take his first good look at the female who was his mate. She had long, light-brown hair that she wore loose around her shoulders. She was the perfect height to tuck her head under his chin when he held her against his chest. Her hazel eyes were wide and filled with fear, but that didn't take away any of her beauty. His cock stirred to life for the first time in two thousand years.

He slowly walked toward her, which had a whimper pushing out of her. Even though she was scared of him, Brolach didn't stop until he stood directly in front of her. He shifted back to his human form, thinking she'd find it easier to handle.

He took a deep breath. Her scent filled his lungs and head. He found it intoxicating, and it set off his werewolf's senses. His wolf side recognized her as his mate along with the vampire. She was his. A mate. The first woman he'd ever wanted to claim.

Brolach reached out for her only to have her suck in a lungful of air and then let it out in a high-pitched scream.

That didn't bother him so much as how fast her heart beat. The sharp, bitter scent of her fear grew stronger. As she opened her mouth to scream again, he caught her chin in his hand and forced her to look him in the eyes.

With his vampire ability to compel lacing his words, he said softly, "You'll no longer fear me. You're perfectly safe. No harm will come to you. We'll leave this place, and you'll take me to your home to provide me food and clothing."

All at once, she calmed. Her heart beat at a normal rate, and the scent of fear blew away on the slight breeze. She nodded as her gaze remained fixed on him. "Okay," she said, sounding in a daze.

"What's your name?"

"Waverly."

"I'm Brolach."

"Brolach," she repeated in the same dazed voice.

"I'll release you now. No more screaming. You'll always feel safe with me."

He stopped compelling, releasing the hold he had over her mind. Waverly blinked a few times, coming back to herself. Brolach hoped never again to have to use it on his mate. If there had been any other way to have calmed her, he would have chosen it rather than take her free will away.

Waverly took a deep breath and looked him up and down. "Come on. We'd better get out of here before someone sees you."

Brolach stayed at her side as she headed down the hill. As they walked, he gazed at the landscape around them. It really hadn't changed much over the last two thousand years. He still recognized it as the land where he'd hunted buffalo and deer.

That changed once they reached a path that led to a large graveled space. It was made by man, as had to be the metal beasts that sat inside it. Brolach quickly scanned the area but didn't see anyone else around.

As Waverly continued walking toward one of the beasts, his steps slowed. "What are we doing here? We need to go to your home."

She stopped and looked at him. "If you want to do that, then we have to go in my car." Waverly pointed to the black metal beast she'd headed toward. "It's a lot faster to drive there than it is to walk."

He had no idea what a car was, but he had a feeling he was about to find out. Waverly led him to the black one. She took something out of her pants pocket, pressed on it, and was able to open a part of the car.

Brolach glanced inside as Waverly stood to the side and motioned for him to come closer. There were two places for sitting. The one he stood near didn't have a wheel in front of it. He looked at her, not sure what was expected of him.

"Get inside," Waverly said. "We can't leave until you do." She looked him up and down. "Hold on a second. Let me put something on the seat first. I don't want mud ground into the upholstery."

She went to one end of the car, and another part of it lifted. Waverly took out what looked to be a folded blanket and then closed the opening before she came to his side once again. Brolach shifted out of the way as she bent, ducked her upper body inside, and draped what she held over the seat.

After she finished, she straightened. "There. Now you can get in."

This time she didn't wait to see if he'd comply. Waverly took hold of his arm, positioned him, and pushed on his shoulder until he lowered himself enough to climb onto the seat. Once he did, she ducked in and secured him to it with a wide black strap that came to rest across his hips and up his chest to his shoulder.

Brolach wasn't at all sure he liked being restrained like

that. He decided to let it go for now as Waverly closed him in and then walked around the car and got inside next to him. When she also strapped herself to her seat, he realized she hadn't tried to keep him trapped. He guessed it was part of what someone did while in a car.

He turned his gaze directly in front of him but then just about jumped out of his skin when a loud rumble seemed to come from all around him. His fangs lengthened, and he growled as he frantically looked around for the threat.

"Relax," Waverly said. "I just started the engine. And you can put those fangs and glowing eyes of yours away. You're acting as if you've never been in a car before."

"Because I haven't."

"Okay. Where have you been? Living in a hole somewhere?"

"No, in the ground for the last couple thousand years."

Waverly appeared not to know what to say to that. She shook her head. "You can explain that after we get you cleaned up and fed."

She pulled on a stick that was between them before she held on to the wheel in front of her, and then the car moved. Brolach watched the scenery go by at a very fast rate and was very much grateful he was immortal.

*

Waverly kept glancing at Brolach out of the corner of her eye as she drove toward town. She had no fricking clue what he was, and for some reason, all it'd taken was for him to look her in the eyes and tell her not to be afraid of him and she wasn't. She'd been on the verge of completely losing it, and now she felt comfortable enough around him to take him home so she could feed him and get him cleaned up. It made no sense.

She glanced at him again. Waverly had to admit that under all that dirt there was the makings of a very handsome face. One she found herself attracted to. Even his deep voice did delicious things to her body. As for his jade-green eyes that glowed at times and fangs that grew in size, she was okay with them. Again, it had to be a byproduct of him telling her not to be scared. His clothes weren't exactly what the normal guy would wear either. The shirt and pants looked to be made out of buckskin, and on his feet he wore moccasins. He was dressed in native garb, but she didn't think he was one. It was hard to tell under all the mud. His hair, which was long and covered the tops of his shoulders, was also covered in it.

Once they arrived at her small, two-bedroom bungalow, Waverly parked the car in the carport. Since Brolach hadn't known how to get into it, she unbuckled his seatbelt, got out on her side, and then went around to help him open his door. As he stood in front of her, she couldn't help feeling short compared to his almost six and a half feet.

She motioned for him to follow her as she walked out of the carport and then to the front door. After she unlocked it, she stepped inside. Once Brolach came in behind her, she shut it. He stood in the middle of her entranceway, looking around.

"I guess we should get you cleaned up first before you eat," she said.

"I'd prefer that."

Waverly headed down the hallway that led to the bathroom. On the way, she stopped at the linen closet and took out a towel. Once inside, she pushed open the glass shower door. Considering how muddy Brolach was, it didn't take a genius to figure out she'd be washing the bathtub once he was done showering. She placed the towel on the counter.

"You should have everything you need," she said. "There's shampoo, conditioner, and a bar of soap already inside the tub. I'm going to have to see what I can come up with for you to wear since you can't put your clothes back on until they're cleaned."

She went to leave, but he stopped her by standing in front of the doorway. "Wait. I need you to stay."

Waverly shook her head. "I'd rather not."

"I need your help."

She swallowed as she pictured the number of ways he'd need "help" in the shower. All of them had to do with him naked. She gave herself a mental kick to get her mind out of the gutter.

"I don't know if that'd be a good idea," she said.

Brolach took a step closer so he was toe-to-toe with her. "I don't understand your world. You have to teach me how to live in it."

She looked him in the eyes. "You've never had a shower before, have you?"

"No."

He watched her intently as she thought over what he'd said. If she told him no again, she had a feeling she'd suddenly have a change of heart without knowing it. Somehow, he'd turn things his way as he had at the grasslands. She didn't want that to happen again. Plus, there was a tiny voice inside her mind that reminded her that she more than wanted the chance to see him without any clothes on.

Waverly slowly nodded. "All right, I'll stay, but I'm not getting into the shower with you."

She turned back to the bathtub and turned on the hot water faucet. Once it ran hot, she cranked on the cold until she had the temperature just right. After she had the water spraying through the showerhead, she turned to find Brolach directly behind her.

"You can get undressed now," she said.

As he reached for the bottom of his shirt, Waverly faced the shower once more and busied herself by closing the door near the faucet and then sliding open the one on the opposite end of the tub.

"You get in here," she said without turning to look at him.

She sucked in a sharp breath as he came around her and did as she'd said. Waverly couldn't stop herself from looking. The man had a gorgeous body. There wasn't an inch of fat on him. He was all muscle right down to his taut backside.

"Try to rinse out as much of the mud as you can before you wash your hair."

Brolach did as instructed. He turned and put his head under the spray of water. Waverly just about swallowed her tongue. His front was better than the back. His hairless chest was well-defined and well-padded with muscle. His six-pack abs contracted as he lifted his arms and pushed his hair away from his face as he wet it.

She dropped her gaze even lower and licked her lips. Brolach's cock was semi-hard. Even in that state it was thick and long. It twitched, bringing her back to the task at hand. Waverly jerked her eyes up and found him watching her with a slumberous expression.

Nice. She'd just gotten caught staring at his dick. She focused on his hair to see how much mud remained. Even though it was wet, it was way lighter now that it was mostly free of dirt. He was blond, which meant he definitely wasn't a native. He had a tanned skin tone, but not the color she associated with the local Lakota.

Waverly studied his face. She'd been right. The mud had hidden one that any woman would swoon over. The longer she stared at Brolach, the more attracted she was to him. A throbbing ache built deep inside her pussy as her body stood up and took notice of the naked, heart-stopping hunk in front of her.

Their gazes met and held. In an instant, the sexual tension between them flared to life. Waverly ached to have him fill her, pumping in and out until they both reached ecstasy. Her breathing sped up and became shallow. Her nipples grew taut under her T-shirt. She wanted him. There was no question about that.

The longer she stared, the more turned-on Waverly became. Lost in the moment, she did nothing to stop Brolach when he leaned out of the tub, hooked his arm around her waist, and brought her into the shower with him. She raised her hands to rest flat against his chest, and for the life of her, she couldn't get her brain to function beyond noticing that he still held her close.

"What next? I've rinsed my hair." Brolach spoke in a deep, husky voice.

It took Waverly a few seconds to understand what he'd asked. She cleared her throat before she replied. "You have to use the shampoo to wash it."

She reached for the bottle that sat in the corner of the tub, squeezed some onto her palm, and motioned for him to bend his head toward her. Once he did, she worked the shampoo through the strands. He closed his eyes and made a low growling sound of pleasure, which had her pussy clenching with need.

Waverly silently washed Brolach's hair twice before putting conditioner in it. All that remained to be cleaned was his body. Her mouth practically watered at the prospect of running her hands all over him.

She grabbed the bar of soap, stuck it under the spray of water, and ran it between her hands to build up lather. Waverly started at Brolach's shoulders before she worked her way down to his chest. She continued her downward journey, but he caught her wrist and stopped her before she reached his cock.

Waverly forgot to breathe as Brolach slowly lowered his head toward her. His mouth settled on hers, and she let out a quiet sigh. He used his lips to gently explore hers and then took them in a heated kiss.

He pushed his tongue inside and twined it with hers,

tasting her. She dropped the bar of soap to the bottom of the bathtub and lifted her arms to put them around his neck. She clung to him as arousal pulsed through her. She couldn't hold back her moans.

Brolach pulled away from her mouth and licked and kissed his way along her jawline to the side of her neck. She felt the drag of his fangs there. A shudder of pleasure whipped through her. Waverly turned her head to the side to give him better access. The sharp points of his teeth touched her skin once more.

She gasped as he bit her. There was a short, sharp pain, which was followed by intense desire. As he sucked, with each pull of his mouth, she felt a corresponding sensation deep inside her pussy. A climax quickly built and then tore through her. Waves of pleasure rolled over her, one after another, until her legs gave out on her. Only his strong arms holding her kept her upright. As he continued to feed, her eyes grew heavy and she lost the fight to keep them open.

CHAPTER TWO

Rolach retracted his fangs and licked his bite mark to seal and heal it as Waverly went limp in his arms. He probably should have waited until they were out of the shower before he fed from her, but he hadn't been able to resist. The sound of her heart beating loudly in his ears, and his need for blood, had made him weak.

Now that he'd found Waverly, his mate, he'd only be able to feed from her once he claimed her. Vampires mated for life just as werewolves did. Being only able to tolerate their mate's blood ensured that bond stayed strong. As a hybrid, each part of him would claim her, tying him doubly to her.

He kept Waverly securely against him as he reached back and turned the water off. He'd watched her start it and remembered how she'd worked the metal attachments set into the wall. Brolach pushed open the door and then carried her out of the tub. He reached for the towel and used it to dry as much of her as he could before using it on himself while he continued to hold his mate.

Brolach looked down at Waverly. He'd probably taken

a little more blood than he should have, which explained why she slept. Even now he felt it coursing through him, making him stronger. He could revive her by giving her some of his, but that would put them on the road to being mated. For a vampire, it took two exchanges to have the bond forming. And her being human, it'd also turn her. He wasn't ready for that yet. Unlike him, she'd have all the weakness associated with a vampire.

He carried her out of the bathing room and then headed down a long stretch of hall in search of a bed. He wanted her to be comfortable while her body worked to replace what he'd taken. Once she awakened, they'd need to eat some food.

It didn't take him long to find the room with a bed big enough for the two of them to sleep comfortably. At first, Brolach thought to put Waverly in it still wearing her wet clothing. He quickly changed his mind as he pulled back the covers. The bedding was unlike anything he'd seen before. The thin sheet on the inside was so finely woven he couldn't see the waft or weft lines that made up the material.

Brolach laid Waverly on the floor that was covered in plush fibers. He took off her shirt with no problem since it easily slipped over her head. Her pants' fasteners were beyond him, and he ended up using some of his werewolf strength to rip them open so he could pull them down her legs.

What she wore underneath those clothes that covered her breasts and sex, he left on her. They were only a little bit damp, and he had to admit he liked how she looked in them. They drew a man's eyes while making him wonder what exactly they hid.

He picked her up and put her into the bed. She didn't awaken. Next time he fed from her, he wouldn't take so much blood. His hunger was under control for now. Once he ate, the food would help temper it as well.

Brolach looked down at Waverly as she slept. Kissing her had ramped up his werewolf side's need to claim her as his. All it took was sex, quite a bit of it, to have the mate bond created. It'd snap into place once the female accepted the male as the one for her. He was more than happy to get started on that, but first he needed to acquaint himself better with this new world he woke up in.

* * * *

Waverly came awake and stretched. She wanted nothing more than to roll over and go back to sleep, but something kept her from doing so. *Whack, whack.* She sat up and scowled at the open bedroom door. What the hell was that sound? She heard it again. And if she wasn't mistaken, the water in the bathtub was running as well.

As she grabbed the sheets to flip them off her, Waverly noticed for the first time she was missing some clothes. A quick look showed she was just in her bra and underwear. She had no recollection of taking her jeans and T-shirt off, or of coming to be in her bedroom. It didn't take her long to find her clothing in a pile on the floor close to the bed.

It all came back to her in a rush. She'd been in the shower with Brolach, helping him wash. They'd kissed, and then he'd bit her, and that was all she remembered. He'd *bitten* her. He'd actually sunk his fangs into her neck and drank her blood.

Waverly jumped out of bed and went to pick up her discarded clothes. The T-shirt was wet, same with the jeans. In fact, the pants were no longer wearable since they'd been torn open. Obviously, Brolach had done that. No one else would have ripped them to take them off her.

The same whacking noise reached her ears. Waverly quickly took out a clean pair of jeans and T-shirt and then hurriedly pulled them on. She left the bedroom and followed the sound to the bathroom. What met her sight had her coming to a shocked standstill just inside the doorway. It looked as if a mud bomb had gone off.

"What do you think you're doing?" she asked in dismay.

Brolach knelt at the side of the bathtub with his buckskin shirt in his hand. He'd just given it another whack on the side of the tub and it dripped muddy water onto the floor.

He looked at her and smiled, showing a bit of fang. "You're awake. I thought to clean my clothes while you slept. I started at the small basin, but it wasn't big enough so I switched to the tub."

Waverly looked at the sink to find it smeared with mud, as well as the countertop, before she turned her gaze back on Brolach. "I can see that."

"I thought I'd better get them cleaned since I have nothing else to wear."

She glanced down his body to see he had a towel wrapped around his waist. She had to admit he looked good in it, but he was far too distracting like that. He definitely needed something else to wear or she'd never be able to think straight enough to ask the questions she had milling around inside her mind.

"Stop doing whatever you're doing," she said. "I think I have something that might fit you. My brother lived here for a few months when he was in between places, and he left a couple T-shirts and a pair of sweatpants behind. They might be a little small for you, but it's better than nothing."

Waverly hurried to the spare bedroom, where she opened one of the drawers in the dresser. She took out a black T-shirt and gray sweatpants her brother, Devin, had left behind when he'd moved out six months before. She'd told him about them repeatedly, but he didn't seem to care.

She returned to the bathroom to find Brolach had

turned off the water in the bathtub and now stood beside it. Since he wasn't holding his dirty clothing, she guessed he'd left them in the tub, which was better than on the floor.

"Here, put these on," she said as she held out the sweatpants and T-shirt. "The pants have a drawstring that goes in the front."

Brolach dropped the towel from around his waist and reached for the pants. Waverly got a good eyeful before he stepped into them and yanked them up past his hips. As predicted, they were a little on the short side and fit a bit snug. The shirt wasn't the right size either but was passable.

Waverly nodded. "Let's get you something to eat." She had this almost overwhelming urge to make sure Brolach had food in his stomach. She'd felt the same way about getting him cleaned.

She turned on her heel and walked out of the bathroom, headed for the kitchen. Brolach followed. Waverly quickly set about seasoning the chicken breasts she'd thawed earlier and then put them into the oven to bake. He'd gone to sit at the small table while she worked.

As she peeled some potatoes to boil, Waverly set the conversation up to ask her first question as she worked. "I need you to give me some answers."

"All right."

"You're not exactly human, are you?"

"Correct. I'm a hybrid—half vampire and half werewolf. As far as I know, I'm the only one of my kind."

"Okay. Right about now I should be running from you in terror, but I'm not even close to feeling that. In fact, I have no fear of you whatsoever. You did something to me to cause that, didn't you?"

Brolach gave her an apologetic look. "Yes. I'm sorry, but there wasn't anything else I could think of doing. I compelled you not to run from me, and to take me to your home. You have my word that I won't use it on you again unless it's absolutely necessary."

"Gee, thanks." She just loved the idea that he could take away her free will whenever he wanted. Not. What he deemed necessary might not match what she thought would be. "Well, just make sure it's a life-and-death situation before you do it again."

"I'll do my best."

"Next question. You said you'd been living in the ground for the last two thousand years. How is that possible? Shouldn't you be dead?"

"I'm immortal. A true immortal, which means I'll never die. There's nothing in this world that will end my life. Not fire, not literally losing my head. Nothing. I could have lasted another two thousand years or more buried there before I decided to awake."

Again, Waverly remained calm as if it were an everyday occurrence for her to meet a vampire/werewolf, immortal hybrid. She found it a little unsettling that she wasn't freaking out.

Finished with the potatoes, she put the pot onto the stove to boil and then turned back to Brolach. "Why did you wake up then?"

He met her gaze. There was no mistaking the longing that lingered in his eyes. "You caused my slumber to end."

"Me?"

"Yes. Even though I slept, I could sense and hear the world above me. Your presence brought me awake." He stood and came to stand in front of her. "I've waited three thousand years to find you."

Waverly swallowed and then asked with a squeak, "Three thousand years?" She cleared her throat. "What do you mean you've been waiting for me?"

Brolach reached up and ran the backs of his fingers across her cheek in a caress. "My mate. You call to my vampire and werewolf sides. Only the woman meant to be mine would do that."

She had a sudden case of butterflies in her stomach and found she needed to sit down before her legs gave out on her. Waverly walked around Brolach and took a seat at the table. He sat in the chair closest to her.

Waverly decided to move past the whole mate idea for now. There was something else on her mind that was more serious. "In the shower, you bit me and drank my blood."

He nodded. "I didn't plan it that way. I needed it, and I didn't have the strength to resist taking some of yours. Feeding and sex go hand in hand."

Her face heated with a blush. She knew that from firsthand experience. He'd made her come as he'd sucked at her neck. And she couldn't deny that it'd been a damn good orgasm. Her pussy clenched just at the thought of it.

"Okay, good to know," she said, her voice huskier than she would have liked. "Next time, and I don't know if there will be, give a little warning before you sink your teeth into me."

Brolach gave her a sexy grin. "It *will* happen again. Once a vampire is mated, he or she can only feed from their mate."

Waverly hid the shiver of delight that went through her by standing and going to the stove to check on the potatoes. The water had just come to a boil. She turned down the burner and then adjusted the lid on the pot. She wasn't quite ready to face Brolach again.

Strong arms wrapped around her waist from behind and pulled her against a hard body. He nudged her hair away from the side of her neck with his nose and kissed her there. A surge of awareness shot through her, and she sighed.

"I might have compelled you to get over your fear of me, but how you react to my touch is all you," Brolach said against her skin.

Waverly couldn't deny that. She'd be lying to the both

of them if she did. The attraction she had for him wasn't to be ignored, especially when he held her close like now. His heat surrounded her, and his hard body molded to hers. His cock, which was also hard, nestled against the small of her back. She barely resisted the urge to turn in his arms and rub herself against him like a cat that wanted to be petted and stroked.

She sucked in a sharp breath as Brolach dragged the tips of his fangs down the side of her neck. He nipped her gently and skimmed his hands lower to her stomach. He tugged her tighter against him and rocked into her. That caused a throbbing ache to build inside her pussy, matching her rapid heartbeat. She took her bottom lip between her teeth to stop herself from moaning. It didn't work. A long, drawn-out one escaped her lips as he lifted one hand and covered her breast. He pinched her taut nipple through her shirt and bra.

Waverly could no longer hold still. She moved in time with his thrusts, pushing back to meet each one. Arousal beat through her, heating her blood. Wetness pooled between her thighs. She spread her legs a little wider as he dropped his hand that had rested against her stomach to her pussy. He stroked her, and the need to have him fill her increased.

Brolach kissed up her neck to her ear. He gave the lobe a gentle tug with his teeth. "The scent of your arousal makes me hungry to take you, but I need food first."

His words had her snapping out of the daze of sexual need that had descended over her. Waverly took a deep, shuddering breath and tamped down her desire. She and Brolach moved a little too fast. At the rate she was going, she'd be falling for him before she could get her mind wrapped around what he was.

"Yeah, I don't want to burn the chicken," she said in a husky voice.

Brolach released her and took a step back. She felt the

loss of his closeness but covered it up by opening the oven door to check on the chicken. She busied herself with testing to see if the potatoes were done. They were.

Waverly turned to find Brolach still close, watching. "The food is almost ready," she said.

She turned away and went about taking out plates and cutlery to set the table. Once she finished, Waverly took the chicken out of the oven and then drained the potatoes before she dished them up. She took a seat at the table, as did Brolach.

They ate in silence, him trying to mimic the way she used her knife and fork. Waverly gave Brolach a second helping once he ate everything on his plate. He finished that one with the same gusto as he had the first.

After they were done eating and she'd put the plates into the sink to be washed with the pots and pans later, she led him out to the living room and then sat on the couch. He followed suit.

"Teach me more of your world," he said.

Waverly reached for the television remote. "This might not be the best way to do it, but I think it'll be easier to show you."

She turned on the TV and watched his reaction to it. Brolach's eyes widened, and then he leaned slightly forward as the images played on the screen. He focused solely on it.

"What is this? How did these small people get inside the box?" he asked with awe.

Waverly bit back a smile. "It's called a television or TV. And those people aren't actually inside it."

She went on to explain how a TV worked. She told him the differences between reality shows and make-believe ones along with movies and the news channels. Like a typical male, it didn't take him long to ask for the remote and to be shown how to use it. After a while, Brolach became so engrossed in watching it, she might as well have not been there. She wondered if she'd made a mistake by getting the three-thousand-year-old hybrid addicted to television.

As Brolach flipped through the channels, only staying for a few minutes on one before switching to the next, Waverly decided to do the dishes. It wasn't as if he'd notice she was gone. She hoped the novelty wore off soon. She hated to think what he'd be like once she introduced him to computers and the Internet.

CHAPTER THREE

Brolach found it hard to tear his gaze away from the TV. It was unlike anything he'd seen before. And it showed how much the world had changed while he'd slept. If not for Waverly, he doubted he'd last very long in it by himself. He no longer had the capabilities to function in it anymore. He was like a child who had to learn everything about the environment he lived in.

In some ways the world wasn't as wild as it used to be. In others, it was harsher. Battles were no longer fought hand-to-hand. Warriors were armed with weapons that could be used from a great distance and caused more damage along with loss of life. It was disturbing to him.

He had no idea how long he watched until he noticed Waverly was no longer beside him. Brolach stood and went in search of her. She wasn't in the kitchen, but he saw the washing up had been done, so she had been in there. He headed toward the room where her bed was to be found.

She was there. Waverly sat on the mattress, holding a black rectangle-shaped object. She touched her finger to its surface and ran it along it. He walked into the room before he climbed up next to her on the other side.

She looked at him. "Did you watch enough TV?"

"For now. I came looking for you when I noticed you weren't there."

"You were kind of distracted, so I did the dishes, then came in here to check my emails and read on my tablet for a bit."

Brolach had no idea what any of those things meant, but he'd ask her about them at another time. He'd gotten so caught up in the TV, he'd neglected his mate. He was supposed to be winning her over, getting her used to the idea of him being a part of her life. So far, he hadn't done much of that.

"Well, I am no longer," he said as he inched closer.

"I can see that." Waverly placed what she held on the table next to her side of the bed and then turned back to him.

He shifted in her direction and put his arms around her. He lowered his head and claimed her lips in a kiss. At first, Waverly just accepted his kisses, but it wasn't too long before she returned them and put her arms around his neck. He growled in approval. This was what he should have been doing instead of watching TV.

Brolach swept the seam of her lips with his tongue before he pushed inside. The taste of her ramped up his desire. He took hold of her waist, lifted her, and positioned her so she straddled his lap, facing him. She let out a quiet moan as her pants-clad pussy came down on top of his hard cock.

He rocked up into her, his werewolf mating urge demanding he take her. His vampire side wanted to sink his fangs into her as he sheathed his shaft deep inside her. He wanted her, and he'd have her. She seemed more than willing. She ground herself against his erection, mewling her pleasure into his mouth.

Brolach skimmed his hands around to her front and pushed them up inside her shirt. He found her breasts and cupped them through the undergarment she wore, thumbing her taut nipples. Waverly sucked on his tongue and arched her back to press her chest harder against him.

She lifted her head, breaking contact with his mouth, and looked at him. Her eyes were dilated with arousal. "More," she said. "I need you to touch me more."

His fangs dropped as his desire grew. "I'll give you as much as you want."

Waverly reached for the bottom of her shirt and lifted it off. She tossed it over the side of the bed. Next, she reached behind her back and did something that undid the garment that covered her breasts. That too ended up on the floor.

Brolach gazed at what Waverly had uncovered. The mounds were more than a handful and tipped with pink nipples. He leaned forward and dragged the flat of his tongue across one. She sank her hands into the sides of his hair and held him against her. He didn't need any further encouragement.

He opened his mouth and took a taut nipple inside. She gasped and rubbed her pussy against his cock. He gently bit the tight peak and carefully ran the tip of his fang along it before he sucked on it hard. He palmed her other breast, stroking his thumb back and forth.

The scent of Waverly's arousal filled his nose with each breath he took. His cock grew even harder and strained against the front of his pants. He released her and took off his shirt before he reached for the material at her waist. It had the same type of fasteners like the other pants she'd worn. He gripped the waistband and would have ripped them open, but she stopped him by pushing his hands away.

"You're not going to rip another pair of my jeans beyond repair," she said. "I'll show you how to get them off the right way. Watch and learn." Once he set his gaze at her hands, she pushed the metal disc through the material. "You undo the button." She grasped a small tab just under the button and pulled down, opening the jeans as little teeth separated. "And unzip the zipper. Now they can be removed."

Brolach took hold of the loosened waistband and tugged it down Waverly's hips. She rose onto her knees and helped him push her jeans past her bottom and then off each leg. She tossed them aside.

He touched the silky material of the garment that covered her pussy, the only thing keeping her from being completely naked. "What do you call this?" he asked in a husky voice as he trailed a finger along the top of them.

"They're my panties, or underwear."

"And what you wore over your breasts?"

"That was a bra."

"I have to say I like them."

Waverly smiled. "Most men do."

"I think I'd like to see you without your panties right now."

"That's doable." She made short work of removing them. "Now you seem a little overdressed with your sweatpants on. They need to go."

Brolach was quick to push down his remaining clothing. His cock sprang free as he tugged the pants from his legs. A bead of pre-cum sat on the very tip. As he tossed the garment away, Waverly used a finger to rub the moisture into his skin. A growl rumbled out of him. Her touch would have easily brought him to his knees if he'd been standing.

He wrapped his hand around the back of her neck and brought her mouth down to his. He kissed Waverly with all the passion that built inside him. She returned it with the same intensity as she fisted his shaft and pumped up and down. His fangs throbbed in time with his erection, but he ignored them. He wouldn't bite her again tonight. This would just be pleasure he could give her with his body.

As she stroked his cock, he reached between them and found her pussy. He dipped a finger into her wetness and then played with her clit. Waverly moaned, and she tightened her grip on his shaft. Brolach pushed a digit inside the opening to her body and pumped in and out. He soon added a second. Her moans increased in volume as she rode them.

"Brolach, you're going to make me come." Waverly panted.

"Not yet. I want to be inside you when you do." He pulled his fingers out of her. "Take what you need."

She released him, held on to the tops of his shoulders, and positioned her pussy over his cock. The head slipped into her wet opening, and they both moaned. With even strokes, she worked his full length inside her until he was seated to the hilt. There was nothing like having his body joined to his mate's.

Waverly rose onto her knees, then slowly sank onto his cock again until he was buried deep. She continued the slow up and down pace as her inner muscles squeezed him tight. Brolach held on to her hips and looked down to watch her pussy take his shaft. He grew even harder.

He drew her closer and nuzzled the side of her neck. Waverly rode him faster as he dragged a fang along her skin. As he edged nearer to his release, the urge to bite tried to take him over. He fought it, concentrating on the pleasure she gave him. He reached between them and found her clit. He stimulated it with the tip of his finger and thrust up his hips to meet each of her downward strokes.

Waverly let out a whimpered moan as she came. Her inner muscles rhythmically clutched and released his plunging cock. Having her fall apart in his arms had his arousal soaring and his balls rising closer to his body in preparation for his own climax.

Brolach kept his arms around her and took her down to the mattress flat on her back while keeping their bodies joined. He lifted his chest off her and balanced his weight on his straightened arms. She held on to his biceps as he surged in and out of her pussy. He took her hard and fast, his orgasm building with each thrust. With a growled groan, it washed over him. His cock pulsed as he filled her with his cum.

Once it was over, he collapsed on top her, mindful of his greater weight. She put her arms around his back and held him tight as they fought to catch their breaths. He was quite happy to stay exactly where he was.

*

Waverly closed her eyes and enjoyed the afterglow. Making love to Brolach could only be described as intense. He'd set her body on fire, and he'd known just how to quench the flame. Boy had he ever. He might be ancient, and had slept for two thousand years, but he definitely remembered how to wring the most pleasure out of a woman. Her climax had been the best she'd ever had.

Brolach was heavy, but not to the point where she wanted him to get off her. He supported most of his weight on his bent arms. His face was against her neck, close to where it met her shoulder. He gently kissed her there, which sent a shiver of delight through her.

It reminded her of how good it'd felt to have him run his fangs along her skin. If he'd bitten her, she didn't think she would have complained. Actually, she'd wanted him to do it. The sensation of his sharp teeth coming in contact with her neck had pushed her arousal higher. After he'd fed from her the first time, she'd thought for sure she wouldn't want him to do it again. Obviously, that wasn't the case.

He lifted his head and brushed his lips across hers. "That was worth waiting two thousand years for."

Waverly smiled. "I'll have to take your word on that since I haven't been alive that long. I've only seen twenty-seven, which probably seems like nothing to you."

"Maybe not, but the main thing is I finally found you."

"So you're still sure I'm your mate?"

"Yes. That hasn't changed. If anything, making love to you has reaffirmed that. My werewolf side wants to keep you in this bed and have sex with you until you've fully accepted me as yours and the mate bond forms between us. My vampire side wants to do the blood exchange that will also tie you to me."

"You might be ready for all that, but I'm not sure I am."

He kissed her forehead. "I know. You live in a world where werewolves and vampires aren't supposed to exist. Even before I went to sleep it was getting to be that way. Humans have always had a hard time accepting what they don't understand."

Waverly had to agree with that. If everyone knew supernatural beings actually existed, there would be riots in the streets. Plus, there was a good chance they'd try to wipe those two races off the face of the earth.

"I might still find it a bit of a shock to know what you are, but I think I'm well on my way to understanding," she said with a smile.

Brolach grinned. "I'm glad."

She grew serious. "Can I ask you a couple questions?"

"Of course. Anything. You're my mate."

"All right. First question. Why were you buried for two thousand years? Couldn't you've found a better place to sleep? Like a cave or something?"

Brolach rolled to his back and took Waverly with him so she lay sprawled across his chest. "I didn't put myself in the ground. I was buried with the hopes I'd eventually die."

Waverly slid off him and sat up at his side. "What? Someone tried to murder you?"

"Not a single someone. It was more than one person."

"Why?"

"Because of what I am. A hybrid. My mother's people, the vampires, believe it's an abomination for one of their kind to mate or breed with a werewolf, which they consider to be animals."

"Obviously your mother didn't think that way."

He smiled. "No, she didn't. She loved my father with all her heart. Since they knew their mating would cause problems with her kind, my parents left their homeland and crossed the ocean on a trip that hadn't ever been done before. My mother was already pregnant with me at the time. After they arrived here, they met the native people, who'd never seen a vampire or a werewolf before, let alone someone with white skin. They took my parents in and treated them as if they were from the gods."

"Where did they come from?"

"A land very far to the north where winter came earlier and lasted longer. During the warm months, the sun never set. And in the colder ones it never rose. My parents called the land Suomi."

Waverly shook her head. "I've heard of that name. I dated a foreign-exchange student in high school. He was from Finland. Suomi is Finnish for Finland. When did your parents come to South Dakota?" At Brolach's blank stare, she added, "When did they come to these lands? They're called South Dakota now."

"Three thousand years ago. I was born here."

"Holy crap. Your parents pre-dated the Vikings coming to North America by two thousand years. That means *they* were the first white people to find the continent."

"You speak of things I don't understand."

"Your parents coming to these lands, being the first

non-natives, it's a big deal. And if it became common knowledge, it'd change history."

"That wasn't their intent. No one knew for sure if there was actual land to be found across the ocean. They were willing to take the risk to live in peace. It was particularly hard on my mother. They made the trip in the summer. Vampires can't survive in the sun. My father built a coffin for her to sleep in when it was light. Many of her kind had traveled that way."

"I guess that's where the myth of vampires having to sleep in coffins comes from. So they came to live with the natives. Did something happen between your family and them to cause you to be buried?"

"No. The natives had accepted us. What my parents didn't count on was some of my mother's family finding out about their mating and where they'd run to. We'd lived here for a thousand years with nothing to fear. That changed when the vampires, my mother's kin, arrived on these lands. They used their blood tie to my mother to find us." Brolach's face grew grim.

"What happened?"

"They took us by surprise one night and set our home on fire. My mother was still awake and smelled it before the flames spread too much. We ran outside to find five vampires waiting for us. My father would have fought them, but they'd subdued my mother and threatened to kill her if he didn't allow them to tie him with ropes that had silver in them. The metal considerably weakens a werewolf. They said they'd let her go if he complied. He quickly agreed since my mother was in the last stages of her second pregnancy. I handed myself over as well, even though silver has no effect over me."

From the harshness in Brolach's voice, Waverly had a feeling the end of this story wasn't going to be good. "They didn't let your mother go, did they?"

He growled. "No. Once they bound my father and me,

they put a stake through my mother's chest to render her unable to move, then set her on fire. My father tried to get to her, but the ropes left him too weak. They took his head while his mate and unborn child burned."

"And you they buried alive," she said softly.

"Not before they tried to take my head too. They didn't know I can't die. As their swords cut through my neck, it healed instantly after the blade passed through. It took them three attempts before they gave up. That's when they decided to bury me with the hopes I'd starve. In shock over my parents' death, I let them."

Waverly swallowed past the sudden lump in her throat. She couldn't image what it'd feel like to have someone try to behead her three times. Brolach had survived it, but it had to have hurt.

"What do you mean you let them?" she asked.

"I'd just lost the two people who'd meant everything to me. In my shock and grief, I lost the will to fight. They kept me bound in the ropes threaded with silver, thinking they were my weakness. They took me to the hill on the grasslands, dug a deep hole, laid me in it, and filled it in. I went to sleep, but it wasn't an ordinary one. I couldn't bring myself out of it. I could hear the world above me. Time moved on, and still I slept. Until you came."

Waverly leaned over and kissed Brolach, knowing if it'd been her to go through all that she wouldn't have come out of it sane. "How did you not lose your mind from lying there bound for centuries?"

He reached up and tucked some of her hair behind her ear. "The ropes eventually rotted off, but I could have broken free at any time. As I said, I was able to hear the world above when someone came near. I listened, and as the language they spoke changed, I learned it."

"That would answer the second big question I had about how you understand English."

"Now I have you to teach me about this world I find

myself living in."

Waverly couldn't get the mental picture of what Brolach had gone through that horrible night out of her mind. To see his parents killed like that in front of him would be devastating. And to lose an unborn sibling on top of it made it even worse. Thoughts of the baby had her mind going down another tract.

She sat straighter. "Brolach, you say because you're a hybrid you're a true immortal and that you can never die, right? Were you born like that or did you have to grow into an adult first?"

"You're correct about the first thing you asked. As for the other, my parents said I was immortal from the day I was born."

"Wouldn't your unborn brother or sister be the same since he or she was a hybrid too?"

He sat up next to her. "Yes. What are you suggesting?"

"Couldn't he or she have survived, even though your mother died in the flames? You said your mom was in the last stages of her pregnancy. A baby can be born early and live. Your brother or sister would be immortal. I'd say the possibility of he or she not dying from the fire would have been great."

"You think the baby lived even as my mother's body burned to nothing around him or her?"

"They tried to cut off your head, and you healed instantly. You were born immortal, and more than likely you were from the instant of conception. A sibling would be exactly like you."

Brolach's face took on a pained expression. "If you're correct, then I left a helpless, immortal babe out in the world unprotected. I was the only one of my family who survived. It was my responsibility to look after my sibling."

"Don't beat yourself up about it. You weren't exactly thinking straight right then. You'd just horrifically lost your parents. Hopefully, some of the natives would have come to investigate the fire and found the baby."

"They more than likely would have. And I'm pretty sure my mother's kin left these lands right after they buried me to return home. As they shoved earth over me, they spoke of having their human servants set sail once they reached the shore and the tide came in."

"If that happened, he or she could be living somewhere in South Dakota." She chuckled. "Lemmon isn't a large town, by any means. There could be a chance I already know him or her if your sibling lives around here. It wouldn't be too hard for an immortal to hide the fact they're not aging by moving to a different town or city when people would notice they weren't."

"I'd be able to recognize another hybrid by scent, just as I can a werewolf or vampire. With the kin blood tie, I'd sense a sibling in the area now that I'm awake. Before he or she would have had to be on top of the hill above me for me to sense them."

"I know the perfect place for you to scope out people. I work at my family's coffee shop. A lot of the townspeople are in and out all day. My next shift is on Monday, two days from now. I'll bring you with me. My dad has been saying he wanted to hire someone to help clear the tables and wash the dishes. You should be able to handle that."

"If you think I can, I guess I'll try. It should give me a better opportunity to sense if another of my kind is in the area."

"Then it's settled. That means we'll be going clothes shopping for you tomorrow."

CHAPTER FOUR

Waverly came awake the next morning on her side in a strong embrace and a hard cock nestled against her backside. She and Brolach had made love twice more once he'd told her about his past. They'd eventually fallen asleep after that.

She bit back a moan as his hand traveled up her chest to one of her breasts, and he tugged on her nipple. One touch and she grew instantly wet for him. She doubted she'd ever stop wanting Brolach. Being in his arms felt as if it was where she was always supposed to be. He may have compelled her to take him with her away from the grasslands, but he wouldn't need to do that again to have her keep him at her side.

Just a night of being in his arms and making love to him, and Waverly had gone and done it. She'd fallen for him—hard. She didn't know if it was because they were fated to be mates or not. All that mattered was that she had. She'd allowed a three-thousand-year-old hybrid to take possession of her heart.

She had no idea how they'd manage to be together

37

since Brolach was an immortal and she wasn't, but right at that moment, she didn't care. All that mattered was what he did to her body that instant. After caressing her breast, he skimmed his hand down her stomach to her pussy.

A finger pushed inside and stroked in and out. Waverly could no longer just lay there. She rode the digit, matching the pace Brolach set. A second soon joined it, stretching her as they plunged as deep as they could go. His cock jerked against her, causing her inner muscles to clench in need.

"I can't complain about waking up this way," Waverly said with a gasp as he used his thumb to stroke her clit.

"Good, because I need to be inside you again."

She had no problem with that. She ached for him to be there. "Then don't make me wait."

He pulled his fingers out of her and then hooked his arm under one of her legs to spread her open. He thrust his hips against her, his cock sliding along her pussy, coating it with her wetness. Once he had her moaning, he pushed the head inside, taking her from behind. He retreated before he pushed forward again, going deeper.

Brolach continued the slow in and out until she'd taken his entire length. He held her around her waist, keeping her tight against him, and thrust harder into her. Waverly pushed back to match the pace he set. She loved the way he stretched her, filled her.

He nudged her hair away from the side of her neck as he rocked into her. He skimmed the sharp tips of his extended fangs across her skin. It ramped up her arousal even more. Every time they made love, she could tell he resisted biting her. He'd nip her, but never enough to draw blood. He'd stiffen, and his breath would become harsher just as it did now.

She reached behind her and cupped the back of his head to keep him from pulling away. "It's okay. You can bite me."

He groaned. "Are you sure? I won't just bite you. I'll feed."

"Do it. I want you to."

Brolach let out a growl and sank his fangs into her. The jolt of sharp pain quickly gave way to intense pleasure. He plunged into her faster, his cock growing harder, as he sucked at her neck. Waverly couldn't hold back keening moans. Her climax gathered steam until it tore through her. Her pussy clutched and released the thick erection that continued to spear into her.

His hold on her tightened to the point where she almost couldn't breathe as he followed her into release. He drew harder at her neck, which sent her into another intense orgasm. She could only ride through it. And still he fed, drawing out her pleasure.

As Brolach retracted his fangs and swiped his tongue across her skin where he'd bitten her, a sense of weakness washed over Waverly. She dropped her arm from the back of his head and fought to keep her eyes open. Blackness threatened to take hold of her.

"Waverly?"

His voice seemed to come from a long distance away. She didn't have enough energy to answer him. The black void called to her, and she didn't have the strength to resist for much longer.

He pulled his softening cock out of her before he positioned her so she lay cradled against his chest and across his lap. She blinked, trying to stop her eyes from closing. He stared at her with a determined expression.

Brolach lifted the inside of his wrist to his mouth and tore it open with his fangs. He kept her head propped up as he placed the wound against her mouth. "Drink. I took too much blood."

Waverly didn't have the will to resist. She closed her lips over his wrist and sucked. As Brolach's blood passed over her tongue, she didn't find it unpleasant. He actually tasted pretty damn good. She forgot it was blood. She drank as she wrapped her hands around his thick forearm to hold him to her. With each swallow, her strength returned and the blackness that had crept up on her receded.

She barely heard him moan in pleasure as she kept drinking until his blood stopped flowing. Waverly let him go and met his gaze. His eyes glowed, something she noticed they did with intense emotions.

"How do you feel?" he asked.

"Great. I can feel your blood racing through my veins. And I like it. Even though the idea of drinking from you should make me very uncomfortable, I want to do it again."

"Not until you're ready to be tied to me permanently. The second blood exchange is all that's needed to have it happen."

Brolach was right. Waverly wasn't quite ready to take that giant step, but with how quickly their relationship seemed to be forming, she doubted she'd feel that way for very long.

She sat up and kissed him. "I do need some time. I haven't even known you for a day yet." She kissed him again before she climbed off the bed. "I need a shower, then we should get you some new clothes."

He came to stand beside her. "I'll shower with you."

Before she could say anything, he scooped her up into his arms and carried her toward the bathroom. There, they made love again until the water ran cold, forcing them to get out.

* * * *

Brolach sat in the passenger seat of Waverly's car, which she called a sedan, as they headed to the store where there would be some clothes for him to wear. He had on the sweatpants and T-shirt that were her brother's. On his feet were the moccasins he'd been buried wearing. Apparently, they'd be getting different footwear as well.

It wasn't long before Waverly brought the car to a stop. She shut off the engine, removed her seatbelt, and looked at him. "We'll get you some new clothes, then go to my family's coffee shop. I figured I'll introduce you to my dad and talk to him about that job opening. That way it'll be all arranged before tomorrow."

"Okay."

He managed to get out of the car without any help from Waverly. Before they'd left her home, Brolach had asked enough questions about the sedan to learn all there was to know about it. He needed to fit in to this new world as fast as he could. And from what she'd told him, just about everyone had cars.

He came to stand next to Waverly and looked around. She'd told him this was the main street of the town. Buildings lined either side of it. He walked beside her as she headed toward one of them.

Inside were different articles of clothing for men. There were T-shirts and sweatpants similar to what he already wore. He also recognized jeans like the ones Waverly had on, only bigger.

He followed her as she went to a section where jeans hung in a row and picked out a couple. "I'm guessing at the size," she said. "You'll have to try some on, but before you do that, we'll get some shirts as well."

Brolach let Waverly choose the clothes. Once he held several in his arms, she ushered him into a small room and then shut him inside after she told him to put on each item. Even though she'd said she'd guessed at his size, everything she'd chosen fit. At her request, he came out wearing a new pair of jeans and T-shirt.

She nodded when she saw him. "You'll definitely fit in the modern world now, looking like that. We just need one more thing to make the outfit complete."

He was pleased that his mate approved. He had to admit that he found the new clothing comfortable now that he wasn't wearing some that were too small.

With the other clothes in hand, she led him to another part of the store. "Now for some shoes."

She grabbed what she called a sneaker. It resembled what she had on her feet. It took a couple tries before they found some that were big enough and didn't pinch. Brolach thought his moccasins felt better on his feet, but he would wear what Waverly thought was best.

She smiled once he finished tying his sneakers. "You're all set."

Now that he had everything Waverly thought he'd need, she paid for the items they'd selected. She used something called a credit card. Apparently, the people in this modern world used either money or credit instead of trading for what they needed. It was a new concept for him.

Brolach carried the bags with all his new things to the car and then climbed in. Waverly drove a short distance before parking behind another building. They got out. He assumed this had to be her parents' coffee shop. And was soon proved correct.

"This is where I work," Waverly said. "My parents' shop."

As they walked to the door, he looked inside the large glass window at the front. There were quite a few people inside, sitting at tables, eating and drinking.

He followed Waverly inside. More than one person greeted her as she walked by, heading toward the back of the large open room. Brolach received curious stares as he kept pace with her.

Waverly stopped in front of an older man who stood by a door. Through the small window in it, Brolach saw people moving around on the other side. He turned his attention back to the man. He shared enough of Waverly's features that Brolach guessed he was her father.

"Hi, Dad," she said as she kissed the older man's cheek.

"Waverly, what are you doing here? Not that I'm unhappy to see my daughter."

"I wanted to introduce you to someone." Waverly reached back and took Brolach's hand. She tugged him closer so he stood at her side. "This is Brolach. I told him about the job opening here."

Waverly's father looked Brolach up and down. "Nice to meet you, Brolach. I'm Trevor. I don't think I've seen you around before."

"I've only been here since yesterday."

Waverly jumped into the conversation once again. "Brolach is from Nebraska. He's just moved to Lemmon." She paused. "I guess you could say he's my boyfriend."

Trevor turned his gaze to his daughter. "Your boyfriend? How did you two meet? It couldn't have been that long ago, since it was very recent when you broke up with James."

"Brolach and I met online. He decided to make the move so we could meet in person and be closer to each other."

"Did he find a place to live yet?"

"He's staying with me."

Trevor scowled and looked at Brolach. "Just give Waverly and I a few minutes to talk."

Waverly's father took hold of her arm and steered her through the door behind him. Once it shut, Brolach followed them with his gaze as they stepped a short distance from it. With his sensitive hearing, he was still able to hear everything they said.

"Waverly, what are you thinking?" Trevor asked. "You met this man on the Internet, and when you see him for the first time in person, you're letting him live with you? I think you're taking an awful risk."

"Dad, it's fine. I know it sounds crazy, but I trust Brolach. He'd never do anything to hurt me. Plus, he'll make sure James stops bugging me."

"Well, that'd be a good thing. I don't like how attached James is to you, even though you're no longer together. He came in here yesterday looking for you. He knows you don't work Saturdays."

"Let's just say he found me, and Brolach set him straight. I doubt James will come around asking for me again. So, will you give Brolach the job?"

Trevor glanced through the window. Brolach met the other man's gaze. If Waverly's father said no, he wouldn't feel bad about compelling him to change it to a yes answer.

Waverly's father appeared to think it over before he nodded. "All right, Brolach can have the job, only because you asked me. That way it'll give me a chance to get to know your new boyfriend. He can start tomorrow on your shift."

"Thanks, Dad. I appreciate it. We'll be here. Tell Mom I said hi."

Waverly gave her father another kiss on the cheek before she walked through the door to join Brolach. He fell in beside her as she kept walking.

"You have the job," she said.

"I know. I heard."

She glanced at him and shook her head. "I forgot how good your hearing is. Then you know you start tomorrow."

"Yes." He decided to keep the compelling option he would have used to himself.

As they reached the door, it was opened by a man on the outside. Brolach took a deep breath, recognizing the stranger's scent as that of a werewolf's. Their gazes met and held. The other man's nostrils flared as he scented Brolach. The stranger's eyes slightly widened, and he wore a shocked expression for a split second before he smoothed his features once more.

"Hey, Cameron," Waverly said with a smile.

"Hi, Waverly," Cameron replied. "I don't normally see you here on Sunday."

Waverly nodded in Brolach's direction. "I was getting my new boyfriend, Brolach, a job. He moved here the other day."

Cameron glanced at Brolach before his gaze settled on Waverly again. "I guess I'll be seeing him a lot since I come to the coffee shop every day to get my daily fix."

She chuckled. "Yes. I'd better let you get inside before you start going through withdrawals. See you later, Cameron."

"Yeah, see you." The werewolf met Brolach's gaze. "And see you around, Brolach."

Brolach smiled wide enough to flash a bit of fang, put his arm around Waverly's shoulders, and tugged her up against his side, showing she was his. "Yes."

Cameron walked around them and into the coffee shop. Brolach guided Waverly outside. He glanced over his shoulder at the other man. He now knew there was at least one werewolf living in Lemmon. There had to be more, unless Cameron had gone lone wolf.

Once they were at the side of the building and headed toward the car, Brolach asked, "Do you know Cameron very well?"

Waverly turned her head and looked at him. "Kind of. He moved to Lemmon about six months ago."

"By himself?"

"Yeah. Why?"

"He's a werewolf. I wonder if he's a lone wolf or if his pack is here as well."

Waverly stopped at the passenger side of her car and gave him a shocked expression. "Cameron is a werewolf?"

"Yes. I can tell by his scent. And he definitely knows I'm not human."

"Damn. I had no idea. What are you going to do about him?"

"Nothing. I'll wait and see if he makes the first move. If he does nothing, I'll do nothing. At least I now know there's one werewolf in town."

"Well, it looks as if the coffee shop was the right place to start your search to see if you have a sibling around."

"Yes. We'll just have to wait and see."

* * * *

After the waitress brought Cameron his cup of coffee and a doughnut, he took out his cell phone and made a call to one of the numbers in his contact list. It rang four times before it was finally picked up.

"Hey, it's Cameron. I've got some news for you. I'm still in Lemmon, and I just ran into a hybrid. His name is Brolach. He's new in town. I think you need to get here as soon as you can." He waited while the person on the other end spoke. "It won't be too hard to keep an eye on him. He's going to be working at the local coffee shop. And I think he's found his mate." He paused again and listened. "All right. I'll see you in a couple days."

Cameron ended the call and then put his cell back into his jeans pocket. He picked up his coffee and took a sip. It was a good thing he liked coming there, and the food, because he'd be hanging around a lot more than he had been.

CHAPTERFIVE

In the late afternoon, Waverly stood at her kitchen table, chopping vegetables to put into a stew she was going to make for dinner. Brolach sat in the living room, watching TV.

After they'd arrived at her place, she'd made them some sandwiches for lunch. Once they were done eating, Brolach had asked her to tell him more about the modern world. He'd had so many questions, and she'd done her best to answer them. One explanation led to another and then another. She had a feeling he had a hard time taking it all in. If it'd been her who'd awoken after a two-thousand-year sleep, she would have found herself overwhelmed.

Their talk had been informative for Waverly as well. She now had a good picture of what life had been like in South Dakota way back then, before the white man had come and settled on these lands. Since Brolach was born there, he'd known no other way of life except for the native one.

From the angle where she worked, she had a perfect view of his profile. He was so utterly gorgeous it almost hurt to look at him. The longer she spent with Brolach, the stronger her feelings became. She was now used to having him around.

Waverly sucked in a sharp breath at the stinging sensation across her index finger. Paying more attention to Brolach than to what she was doing, she'd cut herself. She put down the knife and brought the digit closer to take a better look. Blood flowed faster as she squeezed it.

She turned to go over to the sink and rinse it under the tap, but Brolach was suddenly there. He'd moved so fast she hadn't tracked him. She let out a surprised gasp.

"You're bleeding," he said as he took hold of her finger.

"Yeah. I stupidly wasn't paying attention to what I was doing and cut myself."

"Let me take care of that for you. My saliva heals."

She'd known that already. He'd bitten her twice, and there weren't any marks on her skin to show he had. Each time he'd finished feeding, she'd felt the sensation of him dragging the flat of his tongue across the punctures his fangs had made.

Brolach brought her finger to his mouth and slowly swiped his tongue across the wound as he held her gaze. It healed in an instant. She shivered as a wave of desire washed over her. Waverly's breath caught as he continued to lap at her skin until all traces of blood were gone. His eyes glowed, which told her he wasn't unaffected by what he did. He'd definitely gotten to her. She was completely turned-on.

His fangs had extended and gently scraped against her skin with his last lick. He tugged her closer and captured her lips in a heated kiss. She went willingly into his arms. Waverly rubbed herself against him and moaned at the sensation of his hard cock nestled along her belly.

She sucked on his tongue as he pushed it into her mouth. She detected the slight coppery taste of her blood. Waverly reached between them and cupped Brolach's erection. It twitched in her hand. She had the sudden urge to get very up close and personal with it.

As she continued to return his hungry kisses, Waverly worked on undoing his jeans. She already knew he was going commando since she hadn't bought him any underwear. Brolach had vetoed them at the store after she'd explained what they were. It was just one less barrier to her prize.

After she parted the material, she tugged the pants down low enough on his hips to spring his cock free. Waverly took hold of it and pumped up and down. Brolach moaned against her mouth as he thrust into her grip. Her pussy clenched as wetness gathered inside it. She didn't think she'd ever get enough of making love to him.

Waverly pulled away from Brolach's mouth and then kissed the hollow of his throat as she lifted the bottom of his T-shirt to his chest. He quickly took hold of it and pulled it all the way off. She placed a trail of wet kisses down to his defined pecs. They rose and fell at a fast rate with his harsh breathing.

She ran the flat of her tongue across each of his nipples before she continued her downward journey. Lower and lower she went, skimming her mouth along his washboard abs until she was on her knees in front of him. She looked up to see him staring.

"Waverly, I don't know how long I can wait to be inside you."

"You'll manage. I've been dying to do this since last night."

She set her gaze on his cock, which was right in front of her. It stuck out straight from his body and was fully engorged. A bead of pre-cum dripped from the very tip. She flicked her tongue out and licked it off. He reached behind him, took hold of the edge of the kitchen table, and leaned back against it.

Waverly wrapped her fingers around the base of his

cock before she licked more pre-cum off the tip. She swirled her tongue around it, paying extra attention to the sensitive spot just under the flared head. Brolach let out an animalistic growl.

She gave him one last lick before she opened her mouth and took his shaft inside. She slid him in as far as she could manage, sucking hard. She pulled back so her lips were just around the tip. After that, she set a steady pace, taking him in and out. What she couldn't manage, she stroked with her hand.

Brolach thrust his hips, his cock growing even harder. "That feels so good."

Waverly moaned along his shaft, which had him growling again. She slid him faster in and out of her mouth. Wetness leaked from her pussy into her panties. The sounds of pleasure Brolach made pushed her arousal even higher.

He gently pulled her away from his cock, hooked her by the arm, and tugged her to her feet. With movements faster than any human could hope to achieve, Brolach stripped off her jeans and panties. He lifted her so she was even with his mouth and kissed her, using lips and tongue. Her naked butt landed on the counter a second later.

Waverly frantically kissed him back. Brolach pushed his pants down farther, took hold of her hips, and slid her closer to the edge. He grabbed his cock and led it to her pussy. He rubbed the head through her wetness before circling her clit with it. She panted, ready to beg to have him take her.

Brolach surged forward, steadily working his cock deep inside her. He held on to the edge of the counter and took her in hard thrusts. She put her legs around his waist, matching his strokes as best she could. His growls mixed with her whimpered moans.

It didn't take very long to have her orgasm building. He speared into her, his pubic bone rubbing against her clit each time he seated himself to the hilt. As she fell over the precipice, Waverly leaned forward and bit Brolach where his shoulder and neck met. That caused an instant reaction from him. He howled like a wolf, thrust into her faster, and came, his cock pulsing deep inside her pussy.

Their harsh breathing was the only sound in the house, except for the TV playing in the background. Waverly released her hold on Brolach's neck and leaned back to look at him.

"I guess you liked that," she said as she fought to catch her breath.

He grinned. "For a male werewolf, a bite on that spot, it's a huge turn-on."

"I'll have to remember that. What about a male vampire? What's his weakness?"

"To have his female sink her fangs into him and feed."

"I guess we'll just have to stick to the werewolf weakness since I don't have any fangs."

Brolach lifted her off the counter and held her in his arms. "You know what makes me extremely aroused. I think now it's my turn to find out what does the same to you."

He stepped out of his jeans, which were pooled around his ankles, and headed out of the kitchen. They only made it as far as the living room and couch before his cock was hard once more. He used it to make her beg for release.

* * * *

It was now the second day of Brolach working at the coffee shop. The work wasn't very hard, and he was just happy to be able to be there with his mate. The idea of being separated from her for long periods of time didn't sit well with him. He already loved her, and he was more than ready to claim her. He only waited for a sign that Waverly wanted him to. The need to do the second blood exchange, which would tie her to him and turn her vampire, was so great he'd avoided feeding from her again. Every time they made love it was getting harder and harder to ignore.

What he really wanted was for the werewolf side of him to mate bond with Waverly first. Then there would be no question about her accepting him as her mate. He'd finish the mating the instant after that happened. Turning her would give her immortality, and he'd never have to fear old age would take her from him.

Brolach looked across the coffee shop as he bussed a table. Waverly stood by another table, where Cameron sat, talking. So far, Cameron was the only werewolf to come there. Plus, he stayed for hours at a time, practically until Brolach and Waverly's shift ended. She'd mentioned how the werewolf hadn't done that in the past. He'd usually come in for a coffee and doughnut and then leave as soon as he was done. Now he ordered at least three cups of coffee and had a couple doughnuts.

Waverly's brother, Devin, came to stand at Brolach's side. He had the same light brown hair and hazel eyes as his sister. They definitely looked like siblings. "You better watch it," he said with a chuckle. "You might have some competition over there. Cameron might try to steal your girl."

Brolach knew Devin was kidding. He turned to him and shook his head. "Cameron is no threat. Waverly has better taste than that."

Devin laughed. "You sound pretty sure of yourself. If I were a woman, I'd think Cameron was hot. He has one of those faces that make women pant after him."

Brolach grudgingly admitted Devin was right. Cameron would be considered very handsome. It was a werewolf trait. Their kind was always good-looking.

"I'm not going to comment on Cameron's looks. I'd rather stare at Waverly."

"I'll leave that job to you. That's my sister, dude. I don't look at her that way."

Brolach grinned. He liked Devin and considered him a friend. Waverly's brother was laid-back and joked quite a lot. Actually, Brolach liked her entire family. Yesterday, the first day he'd come to work there, her father had watched him closely, especially when he was around Waverly. Today he hadn't been so vigilant. He had a feeling he was close to being accepted as a part of Waverly's life.

Devin walked away and then headed into the kitchen. He was one of the bakers. Brolach turned his attention back to Cameron and Waverly. Even though he didn't have anything to worry about, he still didn't like how the werewolf tried to monopolize Waverly's attention. It was time Brolach did something about it.

He left the tub of dirty dishes on the table and walked to where Cameron sat. Brolach came to stand beside Waverly and put his arm around her waist. He looked at the werewolf and met his gaze.

"Out back," Brolach said. "Now."

"I'm not done with my coffee," Cameron replied.

Brolach leaned close and whispered, "Don't push me, werewolf. It's time we had a talk."

Not about to let Cameron have another chance to say no, Brolach released Waverly, grabbed Cameron by the arm, and hauled him up onto to his feet. He force-marched him to the entrance. Waverly followed and quickly told her father on the way by that they'd be back in a few minutes.

Brolach didn't let go of Cameron until they were behind the coffee shop where there were no windows. There was also no other building behind it, just a high fence. He walked a short distance away from the werewolf, taking Waverly with him, before he turned to face Cameron with a growl and snarled lip.

"What are you playing at, Cameron?" he asked with another growl lacing his words.

"I don't know what you mean."

"Yes, you do. You know Waverly is my unclaimed mate. My scent is all over her. As a werewolf, you should know to keep your distance."

"As you said, you haven't claimed her yet. She's still free, and human."

Brolach had been walking a fine line when it came to his mating urge. Cameron's words pushed him a little over the edge. Brolach didn't think and shifted to his wolf form. He raised his hackles and growled as the werewolf shifted as well.

*

Waverly could quite easily see this situation getting totally out of hand very fast. There were now two snarling and growling wolves facing each other down. It wasn't something she wanted others seeing. She had no idea how she'd explain why she was in the company of what looked like two wild wolves.

She stepped closer to Brolach and sank her hand into his thick, light brown fur at his neck, prepared to give it a good yank if he decided to go after Cameron. Not that she thought it'd actually stop him.

Waverly knew both of them would understand what she said while they were in wolf form. Brolach had been teaching her about werewolves and vampires.

She cleared her throat. "Would the two of you knock it off?" Waverly turned her gaze on Cameron. "You stop yanking Brolach's chain. Being what you are, you know damn well I'd never be interested in anyone else but my mate." She looked down at Brolach. "And you stop letting Cameron get to you so easily. You have nothing to be jealous of. Now would the two of you shift, please, before someone sees you like this?"

"I think that's a very good suggestion. That way we can all talk."

At the sound of the new voice, Waverly looked past Cameron and found a man and woman standing behind him. It'd been the man who'd spoken. The two seemed to have their gazes locked on Brolach.

The two wolves' bodies blurred and shimmered as they took on their human forms. Brolach took her hand and held it tight. Cameron went and stood a little behind the other two.

Waverly looked at Brolach when he stiffened. "What's the matter?" she asked quietly.

"They're hybrids. Half vampire and half werewolf like me."

She gazed at the two new arrivals and then back at Brolach. She sucked in a breath. Could it be? Both the man and woman had some shared features with her mate, right down to the same colored hair and eyes. She'd thought there was a chance there was only one other hybrid out there, but two?

The man and woman walked closer and stopped a few feet away. The man spoke again. "That's right. We are hybrids. And you, Brolach, are our brother. We've been searching for you for a very, very long time."

CHAPTER SIX

Rolach stared at the two hybrids, knowing the male had told the truth. They were his siblings. A werewolf's scent was made up of a component that marked them as an individual as well as one that all his or her family shared. The newcomers had that and matched his. Plus, they had the family blood tie that vampires had.

"How can there be two of you?" he asked.

"They're twins," Waverly said.

The male smiled and nodded. "Correct. I'm Torger and this is our sister, Kaisa."

"Those were my parents' names," Brolach said.

Torger nodded. "Before we continue this conversation, I think it best if we go to a place where we won't be overheard."

Waverly spoke up before he could answer. She looked at Brolach. "You can take them to our house. I'll give you the keys before you leave."

He didn't miss the fact she'd called the house theirs instead of just hers. He shook his head. "I won't need the keys. You're coming with us. You're my mate, even though I haven't claimed you yet. There's no reason you shouldn't be there with me."

Waverly went on tiptoe and gave him a quick kiss. "All right. Wait out here. I'll make up some excuse for us leaving early that my dad will believe. He shouldn't mind since we only have a couple hours left on our shift anyway."

She hurried away, leaving Brolach alone with the three others. He ran his gaze over his brother and sister. Torger was just as tall as he was and had the same muscular frame. Kaisa was a little taller than Waverly and had a slim build. He found it hard to believe he had siblings, let alone two of them. He thought back to when his mother had been alive and pregnant. She'd said she swore there was more than one baby inside her, kicking her in the ribs. She'd mostly been joking since twins were a rarity for vampires and werewolves alike. It explained why her belly had gotten so large. His father had said she was bigger than she'd been when pregnant with Brolach.

Waverly returned with a smile. "We're all set to go. You guys can follow me to the house."

They headed to the parking lot. Brolach and Waverly climbed into her car, while Cameron got into another and Torger and Kaisa into a third. Waverly pulled onto the street with the other two cars following. So many questions whirled through Brolach's mind on the short trip home.

After they arrived, Waverly unlocked the front door of the house and waited for everyone to come in before she shut it. They went to the living room and spread out on the couch and two armchairs.

Once they were settled, Brolach looked at his brother and sister, who'd taken the armchairs. "You said you've been searching for me for a long time."

"Yes," Kaisa said, speaking for the first time. "We knew you still had to be alive since you're a hybrid, a true immortal, like us." She motioned to Torger.

"How did you know about me?"

"Our parents told us."

"Parents?"

"Kaisa means our adoptive parents," Torger said. "Our father was one of the hunters who came to investigate the fire. He found the remains of our birth parents. He also found Kaisa and me lying in the ashes of our birth mother. He wrapped us in his shirt and brought us home to his wife. They had no children of their own."

"Our parents had known our birth parents and you," Kaisa said, jumping back into the conversation. "We were raised on stories of our true family. How they'd come from the gods, and how different they'd been." She met Brolach's gaze. "When they couldn't find your body, they thought you might have escaped and hid somewhere. All the hunters of the tribe searched for days for you, but never found you. They figured the ones who'd killed our birth parents had taken you away with them." She paused. "It's only been recently that we learned that wasn't what happened to you."

Brolach shook his head. "It isn't. It was vampires who killed our parents. Our mother's family."

"We learned that," Torger said. "It took us many, many years to find out what lands our birth parents had come from, and who had murdered them. A lot of the family have moved to different countries, with quite a few living throughout the States. We've been hunting them down, trying to get the true story of what happened here in South Dakota on the day of our birth."

"I can tell you that," Brolach said with a sigh. "The vampires set fire to our home to flush us out. They captured our mother once she ran outside. They lied and told our father they'd let her go if he surrendered to them. They bound him and I with ropes threaded with silver, then burned our mother at the stake. While she screamed as the flames claimed her, they cut off our father's head. They tried three times to do the same to me, but I healed instantly."

"Fuck," Cameron said from where he sat next to Brolach on the couch. "Three fucking times?"

"What happened to you after that?" Kaisa asked.

"They kept me bound, thinking the silver weakened me, and buried me on a hill in the grasslands. I let them." Brolach paused and looked at his brother and sister. "I went to 'sleep.' If I'd known the two of you lived, I wouldn't have given up." He shook his head. "I didn't awaken until Waverly came to the hill a few days ago. She was the one who suggested I could have a hybrid sibling out there who'd survived the fire that took our mother. It never occurred to me since you hadn't been born."

Kaisa stood and came to stand in front of Brolach before she went on her knees. She took his hands in hers. "You didn't do anything wrong. As you said, you didn't know. We've found each other now. You, Waverly, Torger and I can be a family."

"Hey, what about me?" Cameron asked.

"Sorry. You, Waverly, Torger, *Cameron* and I can be a family." She leaned in and hugged Brolach and then stood and turned her head to look at their brother. "At least we know that snitch of a vampire in Finland was right about Brolach being buried."

Torger nodded. "That also means he could have been right about our mother's family keeping watch over where they did bury him."

Brolach stiffened. "The vampires are here in Lemmon?"

"We're not sure yet. Cameron, who is a very close friend, originally came here to see if he could find any clues left behind that could tell us what happened to you."

Cameron snorted. "After two thousand years, it's been like looking for a needle in a haystack."

Torger smiled. "You know you enjoy it." He turned his

gaze back on Brolach. "He's known for having a knack for finding people. Anyway, we were in Finland up until yesterday. We'd gotten the information about you being buried alive and an estimation of where you were. We told Cameron, who was going to do some searching. The day he met you in the coffee shop was when he'd planned to go to the grasslands."

Cameron chuckled. "You have no idea how shocked I was to run into you and Waverly. I knew from your scent you were a hybrid. With the name Brolach, I would have to be an idiot not to put two and two together. Plus, there's the fact you look like Torger and Kaisa."

"So that's why you've been hanging around the coffee shop so much," Waverly said.

The werewolf nodded. "Torger asked me to keep an eye on Brolach until they could get to Lemmon."

Waverly shook her head. "And to bug the crap out of him by using me."

Cameron shrugged. "What can I say? I was bored."

Torger laughed. "Cameron's boredom has gotten us into a few messes over the years."

Kaisa rolled her eyes. "I've lost count of how many times I've gotten your dumbasses out of them."

Brolach watched the interaction between his brother and sister with Cameron. It was easy to see they shared a friendship that had lasted a great many years. He ached to have that kind of closeness with Torger and Kaisa. He doubted he'd ever forgive himself for not being there for them on that fateful night. He had no idea what would have happened to them if they hadn't been adopted by that native couple.

Waverly laced her fingers with his. "Stop," she said quietly.

"Stop what?"

"The expression says it all. You didn't know they were alive, but now you've all found each other. You have an eternity to be with them."

"You're right."

Brolach leaned toward Waverly and kissed her, putting the love he had for her into it. Once he pulled away, he found the three others in the room watching them.

He cleared his throat. "So, what do we do about the vampires who may or may not be around here?"

"We'll keep an eye out for them," Torger replied. "If someone is watching over where you were buried, they could already know you've awakened. If they do, the ones we really want, those vampires who were the ones to kill our parents, may come to try to finish you off. I'm hoping they do. They need to pay for what they did."

Brolach couldn't agree more. The faces of the vampires who'd ended his parents' lives were forever etched in his mind. He looked at Waverly. If his enemy did come for him, he'd have to do everything in his power to protect her. Even if he turned her, she'd be just as vulnerable as his mother had been. The only way to keep her truly safe was to put an end to the ones who'd threaten her. He wasn't sure if he could survive if something happened to her, if she were taken from him. Even though he knew of no means that would end his immortal life, he wouldn't give up trying. Going to ground and "sleeping" wouldn't work. Not with his mate's passing. Only the finality of death would suffice. Now that he'd found her, he understood why his father had given up so easily after the death of his mate. Life no longer held appeal without the woman you loved in it.

* * * *

It was late into the night before Torger, Kaisa, and Cameron left Waverly's place. Brolach spent a great deal of those hours learning more about his brother and sister. They discussed plans on what to do if there truly were vampires around town. There was a good chance they'd have human servants who'd do their bidding during the day when they couldn't be out. There was no way the others would know who they were. The servants' scents remained human. For Waverly, it was a bit of a scary thought. She wouldn't know who to be wary of.

Alone at last with Brolach, Waverly could tell he was lost in his thoughts. They sat together on the couch, watching television. He hadn't said more than a couple words since his siblings had left. He had a faraway look in his eyes. She decided a distraction was in order.

She turned off the TV with the remote, put it on the table at the end of the couch, and stood. She turned toward Brolach and held out her hand. "I think it's time we went to bed."

He seemed to come back to the present and looked up at her. "I'm not tired yet."

She smiled. "Who said anything about sleeping?"

Brolach put his hand in hers and stood as she pulled him up. She led him out of the living room, down the hall, and into the bedroom. She turned the lights on with the switch before heading to the bed.

Once she reached it, she put her arms around his waist and rubbed against him. "I think we have to do something to pull you out of your thoughts. I know exactly what you need."

He cupped her face and tilted it up. "You do?"

"Yes. Something we'll both enjoy."

"I think I know what that will be."

Brolach bent his head and brushed his lips across hers. Waverly sighed. "Yup, that's part of it."

The kisses they exchanged became more carnal with each article of clothing they took off each other. Once they were naked, Waverly was well on her way to being completely aroused. Brolach lifted her and placed her on the center of the bed before he followed her down. He covered her with his body, his cock coming to rest between her legs, but he didn't attempt to enter her.

He took her mouth once more in a heated kiss. She pushed her tongue inside his and licked each of his fangs, which were fully extended. He moaned. During the many times she'd made love to Brolach, Waverly had found those long canines of his were an erogenous zone much like his cock. She'd also noticed he'd avoided using them on her.

He ran his hand down her side before he hooked her leg over his arm, spreading her open wider. He rocked into her but still didn't join their bodies.

Waverly whimpered with need. She was more than ready to have him take her. It wasn't until she reached down and dug her nails into his ass, trying to tug him forward, did he push the head of his cock into her wet pussy.

Waverly lifted her hips, and Brolach sank deeper. He set a slow and steady pace, which drove her crazy. She wanted him harder, faster, but he had other ideas. No matter how hard she set her nails into his backside, he didn't give her what she wanted.

"Brolach," she moaned. "More."

His upper body held up on his bent arm, he looked down at her. "Not yet." His thrusts stopped, and she groaned in frustration. "Patience," he said. "I need to say something to you."

"Right now?" she asked practically on a wail.

"Yes. It's no better time than now with me buried so deep inside you I don't know where I end and you start." His jade-green glowing eyes looked into hers. "Waverly, I love you. You've given me a reason to stay in the world. Thanks to you, I've found my family."

She reached up and caressed his cheek. "I didn't do much about bringing Torger and Kaisa here."

"No, but if you hadn't come to that hill and awakened

me, I might not have ever met them. For that, I can never repay you, except with my heart. My love."

"Well, you already own mine. I love you, Brolach. I've never felt like this about anyone before. For me there will be no one else."

With a moan, he pulled back and then surged into her. This time he gave her what she wanted. He thrust in and out at a quick pace. He angled his cock so it rubbed the right spot inside her to have an orgasm quickly building.

Waverly held on to Brolach's wide shoulders. Closer and closer her climax came to the surface, her body coiling tight. Her eyes snapped open as a sensation like nothing she'd ever experienced before took hold of her. It was almost as if a piece of him reached out for a piece of her. Almost as if their souls met. Once the two halves wrapped around each other and became one, something instantly formed between them, invisibly tying them together.

It had her hurtling into an intense orgasm as she whimpered Brolach's name. A wolf's howl pushed out of him as he followed her into release. His cock pulsed deep inside her, filling her with his cum.

After he collapsed on top her, Waverly asked, "What was that? I felt something…different."

Brolach lifted his head and kissed her. "That, my mate, was the werewolf part of me claiming you. The mate bond has formed. You're now mine."

"What about the vampire part?"

"It hasn't yet. Not until after we've done the second blood exchange. Then that bond will form, and you'll be turned."

Waverly pushed on Brolach's shoulder until he rolled off her and lay on his back beside her. She sat up. "What do you mean I'll be turned?"

"With the second blood exchange, you'll no longer be human. You'll be a vampire."

"Hold on a second there. You mean like a real vampire

who can't go out in the sun and has fangs?"

"Yes. Plus, you'll be immortal. You just won't have the same true immortality that I do."

"You never said anything about me being turned when you told me about the blood exchanges."

Brolach pushed himself up into a sitting position. "It's the only way we can have forever together. I don't want to lose you to 'old age. I thought you'd want that now that I claimed you."

"I do, but it isn't something I can do without taking my family into consideration. How am I going to explain why I have to suddenly avoid the sun, and that I can only work when it's dark outside? That wouldn't work out too well in the summer when it stays light for a lot later."

"We'll figure it all out once you're turned."

"No, we'll do that before the second blood exchange. This is a big, life-changing step for me to take. I'm not going to do this without thinking everything through. You have to give me more time."

Brolach blew out a breath. "I don't know how much longer I can resist biting you. Now that we're bonded, it'll get even harder. Mated vampires can only feed from each other. Their bodies will reject the blood of anyone else. Being a hybrid, I don't know if that's already come into play for me since my werewolf side has finished the mating with you."

Waverly quickly kissed him. "Well, I don't want you experimenting to find out. I love you, and I do want to have an eternity with you. I only need a few days. That's all I ask."

"All right, but I won't be able to make love to you again until you accept the exchange. You have no idea how hard I had to fight with myself not to sink my fangs into you just now. Your blood calls to me."

"Two days. I promise."

He kissed her thoroughly, his extended fangs gently

brushing against her lips. All too soon, Brolach pulled away with a groan. "I'll wait. I'd never push you into something you weren't ready to accept. I love you too much to make you resent me like that."

Waverly went and turned the lights off before she climbed back onto the bed. "I know we can't make love again, but can you at least hold me while we sleep?"

Brolach pulled the covers down and gathered her into his arms before he positioned them so they lay stretched out on the mattress. He kissed the top of her head. "I'll hold you all night."

She closed her eyes. With her head pillowed on Brolach's chest, the sound of his heartbeat lulled her to sleep.

CHAPTER SEVEN

The next day, Brolach and Waverly were at the coffee shop to work their shift. Before they'd left their house, she'd said she'd talk to her dad about getting them switched off the dayshift. She hadn't come up with a reason, but figured she'd think of something before she talked to him, which she planned to do closer to the time they could leave.

It was close to the end of Brolach's and Waverly's shifts when she came to him while he washed a bunch of dishes in the kitchen. "I'm going to put some of the trash out in the Dumpster, then I'll have that chat with my dad," she said quietly. "He's in his office right now."

"All right."

Waverly gave him a kiss and then headed out the back door with a garbage bag in each hand. The sound of someone pretending to be sick had Brolach turning to look at Devin, who stood near one of the ovens, acting as if he were going to throw up.

"You two are so cute together it almost makes me sick,"

Devin said.

Brolach threw a damp dish towel at Waverly's brother, who easily caught it. "At least we have each other. I don't recall seeing you with a girl. That's right. You don't have one."

"Hey, man, that's a low blow. I haven't found Miss Right yet, but I'm always working on it. Not many women can resist my charm."

He laughed. "I have a feeling you're the only one who thinks that way."

"You're getting better at the trash talk, Brolach."

It was true. He was getting better in tune with the modern world. As for learning how to trash talk, he'd had lots of opportunity with Devin around. He had a feeling it was Waverly's brother's favorite thing to do. Devin did it to everyone he knew, except to his father, who only had to give his son a certain look and Devin shut his mouth.

They continued to good-naturedly rib each other until Devin suddenly grew serious. "Did you see Waverly come back inside? I didn't. It shouldn't take that long for her to take out those couple bags of trash."

Brolach shook his head. "She didn't. Maybe she walked around to the front and came in that way. She said she wanted to talk to your dad."

"Well, that would be a silly thing to do since Dad's office is back here."

The office was in a little room inside the kitchen off to one side. It really would be kind of out of the way for Waverly to walk around the building to come in by the front entrance and then have to go through the coffee shop to reach where her father would be. And she *was* taking longer to return than it should have necessitated. A feeling of uneasiness settled over him.

Brolach headed toward the back door. Devin followed in his wake. He pushed open the door and stepped outside. The area was empty, and he couldn't find

Waverly anywhere. He called her name and was met with no response. His gaze landed on the garbage bags, the ones she'd carried out of the coffee shop. They sat on the ground a short distance from the Dumpster, as if someone had just abandoned them there.

As he walked toward them, he spied a folded piece of white paper stuck to one of the bags. Brolach hurried to it and tore it off before he opened it. Even though he spoke English, that didn't mean he knew how to read it. The note was definitely written in that language. He growled with frustration.

"What is that?" Devin asked as he came to stand beside him.

Brolach held it out to Waverly's brother. "A note. Read it." After the other man took it, he silently scanned it. "No. Read it out loud. I don't know how to read." He didn't even know how to read Finnish. Being able to read had only been for the more learned way back when.

Devin jerked his eyes up and looked at him. "For real?" At Brolach's nod, he shook his head and set his gaze on the paper he held. "Okay. It's addressed to you. It says they've taken your mate, and that if you want to see her again you need to go to your resting place. It isn't signed." He lifted his gaze. "What does this person or persons mean by 'your mate'? And does this have anything to do with Waverly? I'm not liking that she's not back here and the trash bags are just left as if she dropped them."

Brolach knew who the note was from. He scanned the area, still not seeing anything, as he spoke. "The human servants to some vampires have taken Waverly since she's my mate."

Devin snorted. "Vampires, dude? You expect me to believe that crap?"

"Yes. Just as I'm a hybrid who is half vampire and half werewolf."

He gave him a big smile and flashed his fangs. He

didn't bother to explain any more and shifted to his wolf form. Brolach heard Devin's cry of surprise but ignored him. In human form, Brolach's sense of smell was better than a human's, but as a wolf it was even better than that.

Brolach put his nose to the ground and sniffed around the garbage bags, hoping to pick up a scent trail. The scents of two other humans were mixed with Waverly's. No vampire had been there, but he didn't really expect one to have been. It was still daylight. He followed the scents to the parking lot where they ended at one of the empty spaces. Obviously, they'd put her into a car and had driven away. He couldn't follow the trail any farther.

He returned to Devin, who stood where he'd left him, with a look of disbelief stark on his face. Brolach remained in wolf form and padded to him. Since he was larger than a wild wolf, his back reached Devin's waist. Brolach jammed his nose into the hand that held the paper and gave it a good sniff.

"Whoa," Devin said. "Please don't take my hand off. If it's the paper you want to check out, here." He held it out in front of him as Brolach continued to smell it.

It had the scent of one of the humans and a vampire. The latter wasn't as strong, but it was one Brolach would never forget. The vamp had taken part in his parents' deaths. He'd actually been the one who'd tried to behead him.

He shifted to his human form. "I need your help, Devin. I can compel you to, but Waverly wouldn't be happy with me if she found out. I need you to remain calm. If you don't, it could mean the life of your sister."

Devin took a deep breath. "Okay, I won't freak out. Holy shit, you can change into a wolf. I just had to say that. Now, what do you need me to do?"

"We have to get Waverly's cell phone. I know she keeps it in her purse while she's working, which is locked away in her locker."

"That isn't any problem. I know the lock's combination." At Brolach's raised brow, he quickly added, "Waverly gave it to me, just as she has mine."

"All right let's go inside, but I don't want you to say anything to let anyone know that Waverly is missing. You can help me with the cell phone, then finish out your shift as if nothing has happened."

Devin shook his head. "No way. If someone has my sister, I'm coming with you."

"It's vampires who have her. They're stronger and faster than you."

"I don't care. I'm going, or I'll raise the cry that Waverly has been taken."

"Fine, but you'll do everything I say. No refusing."

"I promise."

Brolach and Devin headed into the coffee shop before they went to the area where the staff lockers were located. Devin didn't waste any time in unlocking Waverly's before taking out her purse. He handed it to Brolach, and the both of them returned to the back of the building. They continued on to the parking lot.

He opened Waverly's purse and fished out her cell. He handed it to Devin. "I have to make two phone calls, but I don't know how to use the phone, and I can't read anything on it."

"I hate to say it, but you sound as if you came from the Dark Ages. Everyone knows how to use a cell."

Brolach growled. "When you've 'slept' buried in the ground for two thousand years, this world has to be relearned. I've only been awake for a few days."

Devin's eyes widened. "Holy shit again. When this is over, we're having a long talk about all this." He touched the screen on Waverly's phone a few times. "Okay, I have her contact list up. Who do you want to call first?"

Luckily, Torger, Kaisa, and Cameron had exchanged phone numbers yesterday with Waverly, who'd put them into her cell. If they hadn't done that, Brolach wasn't sure how he'd get in contact with the others. He needed them to help save Waverly. He and Devin wouldn't be able to do it on their own.

"Look for Torger's number."

"Okay. I didn't know Waverly knew anybody by that name."

"He's my brother."

"You say you were buried for two thousand years, yet you have a brother in Lemmon."

"And a sister as well. We'll talk about this later, Devin. Will you please make the phone work to call Torger."

"All right. I'll hold you to that, by the way."

Devin touched the screen of the cell phone once more and then handed it to Brolach. He held it up to his ear and heard a ringing sound coming from it. It rang a few more times before his brother answered.

"Hi, Waverly. I thought you'd still be at work," Torger said.

"It isn't Waverly," he replied. "It's Brolach. I have need of you, Kaisa, and Cameron."

"What's the matter?"

"The vampires have Waverly."

"What? How?"

"Their human servants must have been hanging around the coffee shop. Waverly went to take some trash out back and didn't return. There was a note telling me to go to the grasslands, to my resting place, if I want to see her again."

"They're going to use her to get to you just as they did our father with our mother."

"I know. This time it won't have the same outcome. I'm going to call Cameron as well. I think three true immortal hybrids and a werewolf should defeat them."

"I'll get in touch with Cameron. Kaisa and I are together so you don't have to worry about calling her. Where are you now?"

"I'm still at the coffee shop."

"We'll pick you up. We have about a half hour before it starts to get dark."

"All right. I'll be in the parking lot."

"See you soon."

Torger ended the call. Brolach passed the phone to Devin. "Torger and Kaisa, my brother and sister, along with Cameron, will meet us here."

"Okay. Is Cameron the same guy who comes into the coffee shop every day?"

"Yes. He's a werewolf."

Devin shook his head as he put the cell into Waverly's purse. "Can I just say wow? So, your siblings are hybrids like you?"

"Yes."

"I guess that's all you're going to say about that. Here." Devin pushed the purse into Brolach's hands. "You can hold this. I don't want to be seen carrying a purse, even if it does belong to my sister. I have a reputation to uphold."

It was Brolach's turn to shake his head. "It doesn't bother me. You should make your excuses to leave before your shift ends. The others will be here soon."

"Gotcha. I'll be right back."

Devin dashed to the back of the coffee shop and then disappeared inside. He was only gone for a short time before he came rushing out and joined Brolach in the parking lot once more.

"All set?" Brolach asked.

"Yeah. I also made an excuse for you and Waverly. I don't think Dad listened too closely. He was busy doing the books for the shop. He hates it but won't let anyone else do it."

Two cars turned into the lot. They drove toward them before pulling into empty spaces close by. One was driven by Torger and the other by Cameron. Kaisa sat in the passenger seat with Torger. All three climbed out of the vehicles and came to stand near Brolach and Devin.

Cameron glanced at Devin before he set his gaze on Brolach. "What's Devin doing here?"

"He knows everything now. About you being a werewolf, and Torger, Kaisa, and I being hybrids. He read the note the human servants left for me after they took Waverly. I can't read, remember? He's coming with us."

"Is that wise? He's human. I think he'll be more of a liability than an asset."

Devin opened his mouth, more than likely to complain, but Brolach held up a hand to stop him. He looked at the others. "That may be so, but he's coming with us. Waverly *is* his sister."

Torger nodded. "All right. Let's go. It's going to be dark soon." He turned to Cameron. "I'll take the lead to the grasslands."

The werewolf gave a nod, went to his car, and got in. Torger and Kaisa climbed into the front of the other vehicle while Brolach and Devin got into the back. Brolach placed Waverly's purse on the seat between them.

"I recognize you two," Devin said as he did up his seatbelt. "You came to the coffee shop with Cameron today." He looked toward Kaisa. "I especially remember you, Kaisa. If I'd known you were Brolach's sister, I would have gotten him to introduce us then. I would have asked you out."

Kaisa turned in her seat to look at Devin. "You could have tried, but it wouldn't have happened. Shouldn't you be worried about Waverly?"

"I am. Sorry, this is the way I handle stress. I tend to shoot my mouth off."

"Well, you're doing a good job of that."

Devin leaned toward Brolach and whispered, "I really do think your sister is hot."

"I can hear you, human," Kaisa said. "Hybrids have very keen hearing, as do werewolves and vampires."

Brolach smiled as Devin settled back in his seat and kept his mouth shut. Torger pulled out of the parking lot and turned onto the street. No one spoke the entire drive to the grasslands, which was fine with Brolach. His concern for Waverly took up his thoughts. He couldn't lose her, not now that he'd claimed her.

Once they arrived at their destination, they got out of the cars and then met near one of the beginnings of the trails. Brolach knew where they had to go wouldn't be on it.

"Brolach, do you know where they'll be?" Torger asked.

"Yes. It's a bit of a walk. It'd be faster if we went wolf and ran there."

"Ah, what about me?" Devin asked. "I can't turn into a wolf, remember?"

"You'll ride on my back," Brolach replied. "You can't slow us down. Once I shift. Climb on. I won't be able to speak to you, but I'll understand everything you say."

As Torger, Kaisa, and Cameron took on their wolf forms so did Brolach. He stood by Devin and waited for him to climb onto his back. Waverly's brother looked a little uncertain about the idea, but in the end, he clambered onto Brolach, leaned low toward his neck, and tightly held on to the fur there.

They took off running at werewolf speed. Devin let loose with a "Holy shit!" as they went faster. Brolach took the lead. The sun dipped below the horizon, and darkness started to settle in.

The hill where he'd been buried would give Waverly's captors a good viewing point. They would easily be able to see anyone who approached them from a fair distance. Once he figured they'd come close enough, he led the group to the side where the grass was a lot taller than the rest. It was enough to hide them as they slowed and continued onward.

After deciding they were at an optimal distance,

Brolach gave himself a big shake and dislodged Devin from his back, who landed on the ground on his butt—hard. Brolach quickly took on his human form.

Devin scowled at Brolach and whispered, "You could have found a better way to tell me to get off, you know."

Brolach put a finger to his lips to silence the other man, inched forward, and parted the edge of the tall grass to get a look at the hill. He bit back a growl as his gaze landed on a single vampire, who held Waverly. His two human servants stood nearby, ready to do their master's bidding.

* * * *

Waverly was weak. So weak the only reason she stood was because of the grip the vampire had on her. He'd fed from her, taking too much blood. Unlike when Brolach had done the same, her captor hadn't given her any of his blood, and it hadn't been a pleasurable experience. It'd hurt like hell. She had a feeling she was now walking a fine line. There was ringing in her ears, and she was more than a little lightheaded.

She must have blacked out a bit, because the next thing she realized there was a giant wolf loping up to the top of the hill. She recognized it. It was Brolach. Waverly wanted to shout at him that the vampire had used her to lure him there, but it was too much effort to form the words.

Brolach took on his human form and came to confront the vampire. She fought to pay attention to what they said to each other. It didn't work. Their words sounded muffled as if someone had stuck earplugs into her ears.

She lost touch with what was going on around her again but was ripped back into it at the pain of the vampire tearing into her throat. It didn't last long. All hell seemed to break loose, and her captor was torn away from her, his fangs doing even more damage. The last thing she saw was the world spinning as she dropped like a stone and everything went black.

*

Brolach howled as Waverly fell to the ground, her neck a bloody mess. He hadn't been quick enough to stop the vampire from biting her. And from the way she'd acted, he was pretty sure that hadn't been the first time the male had fed from her.

As he'd gone to confront the vampire alone, Torger, Kaisa, and Cameron had worked their way behind the hill. The vampire wouldn't be expecting two other hybrids nor a werewolf to be with Brolach. They used it to their advantage.

Much to his surprise, the vampire had been the only one of his kind there, which had made the others' job easier. Cameron had easily taken out the human servants, rendering them unconscious, as Kaisa and Torger had pulled a sneak attack on the unsuspecting vampire. It'd worked without a hitch, except for the vamp biting Waverly.

As Kaisa and Torger held on to the vampire, Brolach walked toward his enemy. Devin ran past him to Waverly. With her brother there to look after her, Brolach confronted her captor.

"Now you'll pay for the death of our parents," Brolach said.

The vampire hissed at him. "Don't you mean your parents? My cousin's unborn child perished with her."

Brolach shook his head. "You have to know the two who hold you are hybrids as well. My mother had been pregnant with twins. They were born by fire."

"Impossible."

"Haven't you figured it out yet? Hybrids are true immortals. We will never die. I was buried for two thousand years and survived. Sadly, you won't survive the flames."

After Cameron passed Brolach a wooden stake that he'd taken out of the inside pocket of his jacket, he didn't hesitate to use it. Brolach stabbed it into the vampire's chest to keep him from being able to move. They tossed him into the very hole Brolach had come out of—his resting place. It was only a matter of covering the vampire with dry grass, setting some on fire with Cameron's lighter, and tossing it onto their enemy.

"Waverly! Waverly, wake up!"

The sound of desperation in Devin's voice had Brolach rushing to him and Waverly. Her brother held her cradled in his arms. Her face was drained of all color and her chest barely rose and fell.

Devin looked up at him. "I think she's dying. She's not going to make it."

Brolach went down onto his knees beside the pair. The sound of Waverly's heart weakly beating filled his ears. It slowed even more, and then skipped a beat. She was dying.

Kaisa came to kneel beside him.

"Brolach," she said. "You can save her. You have to finish the blood exchange and turn her. It's the only way."

"I promised Waverly I'd give her a chance to ease her family into it since she'll no longer be able to move about in the day."

"That's not true. We're hybrids. Many years ago, I ended up turning a woman who was a close friend to me. She became a day walker. In every other way, she was like other vampires. Do it, brother. Turn your mate before it's too late."

Brolach looked at Devin.

"Do it," Waverly's brother said. "Save her."

He took Waverly from Devin's arms and held her close. Even though she'd been almost drained, Brolach bit into her wrist and took a small amount of blood. That was all he needed. He sank his fangs into his own and placed it against her mouth.

At first, she didn't do anything. He clenched his fist, forcing the blood to flow faster and into her mouth. It was only a matter of seconds before Waverly moaned and then sucked on his wrist. She reached up, held on to it, and drew on it harder. As she swallowed mouthful after mouthful, Brolach felt his vampire side claim her as a mate. She suddenly let go of his arm and went limp with her eyes closed.

"What happened?" Devin asked. "Did it work? Why isn't she awake?"

Kaisa went and put her arm around Devin's shoulders. "It's fine. It worked. Waverly is in the midst of turning. I can hear her heart beating. She'll awaken shortly."

Brolach held his mate closer and kissed her forehead. He noticed the wound in her neck had healed. As he waited for Waverly to wake up, he watched his siblings and Cameron handle the humans who'd regained consciousness. The vampire no longer alive, the hold he'd had over his servants was no more. It hadn't been something they'd chosen. Torger forced each one to look into his eyes and compelled them to forget their time with the vampire and what had transpired there on the hill. He sent them on their way.

"Brolach?"

He looked down at Waverly. She was awake and looked no longer on death's door. "How do you feel?"

"Better." She ran her tongue over her new fangs. "Do I have fangs?"

"I had to turn you. It was the only way to save you. I know you wanted to wait, but I couldn't lose you."

She smiled, flashing more of her fangs. "I'm glad you did. Dying would have sucked. I'll just have to think of some other way to explain to my family why I have to change how I live."

"You don't have to worry about that for a while. Kaisa turned a human before. Hybrids make day-walker vampires. Once you reach the stage where you should be aging and you're not, that's when you'll have to do some explaining."

"You'll have me to help, sis," Devin said.

Waverly's gaze shot to her brother. "Devin? You know about Brolach and the others?"

"Yeah, and I'm okay with it." He leaned toward her and gave her a kiss on the cheek. "I'm sure you two want to be alone right now." Devin pushed to his feet. "I think I'll see if I can snag the interest of a pretty hybrid."

Waverly shook her head. "He'll never change. He's going to drive Kaisa nuts."

Brolach chuckled. "I think my sister will be able to handle him just fine."

She sat up and cupped his face. "I love you. I'm glad I'm mated to both sides of you. We now have an eternity together, and I plan to show you each day of it how strong my love for you is."

He kissed her hard and long. Once he pulled away, Brolach said in a gruff voice filled with emotion, "I love you, my mate. I waited three thousand years to find you. Nothing will ever tear us apart."

Brolach stood and let Waverly stand. He put his arm around her shoulders and tucked her tight against his side. There were still more vampires to hunt down and end their existence, but that would wait for now. He had something more important to do, like show his mate how good it would be to sink her new fangs into him as he made love to her.

The End

FALLING FOR A HYBRID

Being a loner, moving by herself from a city to a small town, is something Rikki is more than capable of handling. Having a strong hunk who offers to help with the heavy lifting was just an added bonus. And one she couldn't pass up.

Torger had sat at the coffee shop across the street and watched the woman who'd snagged his interest carry boxes out of a moving trailer before he could no longer stay away. His interest in her is a sign his vampire side considered her a mate. Once he had her scent in his nose, his werewolf one agreed.

With his vampire side of the family still hunting him, his sister and brother, Torger knows he puts Rikki at risk, but there is no denying the mating instincts of a hybrid. Even though his closeness to her puts a target on her back.

CHAPTER ONE

Rikki hefted a box out of the rental trailer she'd packed with all her belongings. She'd just moved to Lemmon, South Dakota, and now had the painful task of unloading her stuff into her one-bedroom walkup apartment. It was above a hardware store located on the main street of the small town with a population of just over a thousand.

She walked to the street-level entrance, then climbed the set of stairs to her new place for what seemed like the hundredth time. Her legs burned. It sucked having to move all on her own. Rikki was just thankful the apartment had come furnished. It would have been impossible for her to lug a mattress or couch upstairs all by herself. And it wasn't as if she knew anyone in Lemmon to ask for help.

She still had too much stuff, though. Rikki was an avid reader and had accumulated an extensive collection of paperbacks before she'd made the switch to ebooks. She couldn't bring herself to part with any of them. Now, after lugging the fifth box of them out of the trailer, she regretted that she couldn't let them go.

After setting the box on the floor with the others in her living room, Rikki straightened and stretched her back. It was too bad she didn't have a big, strong boyfriend to carry the heavy items. Sadly, she'd been single for a while.

Rikki headed back outside to the trailer. After assessing the number of boxes that were left, she figured she still had at least another five or six trips to make until she was finished. She took a deep breath. The end was in sight.

Before she stepped inside the trailer, she glanced across the street. Her gaze landed on a man who stood facing in her direction, seeming to stare at her. Even though he wasn't that close, from the distance between them, she couldn't help noticing he was good-looking. Like *really* good-looking. Made her sex-starved body stand up and notice, even though the move had almost drained all the energy out of it.

He looked tall, well over six feet. At least he did from the opposite sidewalk in front of a coffee shop. He had short, blond hair and a muscular body that was hidden in a pair of black jeans and a black T-shirt that hugged it to perfection. *Oh, baby.* Momma liked.

Rikki gave a wistful sigh before she forced herself to tear her gaze off the hunk and get back to work. The boxes weren't going to move themselves up to her apartment, much to her disappointment. Since Lemmon was small, maybe after she was settled in, she'd run in to him and see if she could get to know him better.

She stepped up into the trailer and then walked to the back to retrieve the next box. Rikki had just bent to pick it up when she was startled upright by a deep-sounding voice that came from behind her. She turned around to find the hunk from across the street standing at the doors.

"Sorry. What did you say?" she asked.

He smiled, which had her almost drooling. "I asked if you'd like some help. I watched you make a couple trips so I know you're alone. It'd go faster with the two of us."

"Ah, sure. I guess."

The trailer bounced as he stepped into it. He had to keep his head ducked. He was tall. There was no way he could stand straight. Now that he was closer, Rikki saw his eyes were green. A deep jade-green.

Once he reached her, he held out his hand. "Hi. I'm Torger. You're obviously new in town."

She shook his hand, getting a small thrill from the skin-to-skin contact. "I'm Rikki. I am new. I arrived this morning."

"It's kind of cramped in here. I'll grab these two boxes."

Torger brushed past her, then reached for the boxes. She was about to tell him they were heavy since they held her dishware and pots and pans, but he lifted them as if they didn't weigh a thing. Rikki quickly picked up a box closest to her and led him out of the trailer, then up to her apartment.

She set her box in the living room before she directed Torger to the kitchen to place his two there. After he did, he looked around. The kitchen was attached to the main living space with no doors or walls between the two rooms.

"Nice place," he said. "Did it come furnished?"

"Thanks. And yes, it did. I lived with a roommate in Rapid City. All the furniture was hers, even the bed I slept on since it was a pull-out couch."

"What made you decide to move to Lemmon? It's a lot smaller than Rapid City, and we don't exactly have a nightlife to call home about."

Rikki smiled. "I figured that. The rent is cheaper so I can afford my own place, instead of having to share. I'm kind of a loner. I don't mind the small-town atmosphere."

"Do you have a job lined up? If not, I could ask my brother about any openings at the coffee shop across the street. His wife's family own it."

"Thanks, but that isn't necessary. I work from home."

"Oh, yeah. What do you do?"

"I'm a freelance editor."

"Interesting."

Rikki chuckled. "Not everyone would agree with that. It's the perfect job for me, though. I love books, but I have a hard time coming up with storylines to write my own. So editing is more my thing. Plus, it's a solitary career, which with me being a loner, it works out as well."

Torger grinned. "I'll have to send my sister and sister-in-law over to introduce themselves. Maybe the three of you could become friends. Then you wouldn't be able to say you're a loner."

"They can try, but I'm not guaranteeing anything," she said jokingly. "I used to drive my roommate crazy. I wouldn't leave the apartment for days at a time."

"We'll definitely have to fix that. Let's get the rest of your things out of the trailer."

Rikki nodded, then followed Torger outside. Holy hell, he was hot. And his being a really nice guy just upped her attraction for him. It was looking as if her decision to move to Lemmon was a good one, and not because her rent was cheap. She always had a hard time meeting new people. Maybe living in a small town would rectify that problem.

She'd like to meet Torger's sister and sister-in-law, but it was him she really wanted to get to know better. He hadn't even blinked at her basically telling him she was a book geek.

At the trailer, they stepped inside and headed to the remaining boxes. There weren't too many more. There was one long, flat box she'd had a hell of a time getting in there. It was the brand-new computer desk she'd purchased before leaving Rapid City. It'd been almost too heavy for her to lift. She'd make sure Torger brought that one up to the apartment.

"Can you take this one?" Rikki asked as she pointed to

the flat box.

"Okay."

Torger easily picked it up and then walked toward the entrance. Rikki grabbed a box and quickly followed.

It took them two more trips to empty the trailer. On the last one, Rikki closed it before she headed upstairs with the final box. She expected to find Torger waiting for her to return so he could leave. Instead, he worked on opening the box that held her new computer desk.

He looked up as she stepped inside. "I figured I'd give you a hand with this. Given how flat the box is, I'm guessing there's going to be a lot of assembling required."

Rikki put down what she held in the entranceway, then closed the apartment door. "Go right ahead. I dreaded having to put it together myself. I'm not exactly handy when it comes to doing things like that. I'm pretty sure I'd mess it up and then not be able to figure out where I went wrong."

"Sometimes the directions aren't that clear or there's a step missing."

"True. I'll still owe you at least a cup of coffee."

His gaze met hers. "How about you pay me back by having dinner with me this evening?"

With the way Torger stared at her, a surge of awareness shot through her tired body. Was that interest showing in his gorgeous eyes? Rikki was pretty sure it was and not wishful thinking on her part.

Rikki swallowed back the urge to sigh. "Ah, I'd love to have dinner with you, but I don't think this evening will work. I have to take the trailer to U-Haul and then I should get started on some of the unpacking."

As she came to stand next to him, Torger stood. "How about you return the trailer and I'll get us some take-out? I doubt you'll feel like cooking after moving, and I still have to put your computer desk together."

"You're right. The idea of going to the grocery store to

shop, then having to cook dinner, isn't appealing. I'd end up buying some fast food."

Torger stepped closer. "Then say yes."

"All right. Fine. I'll return the trailer, and you get the take-out. You can meet me back here in an hour."

"You won't regret this. What would you like to eat?"

Oh, she knew she wouldn't regret it. She only hoped she didn't blow it with Torger and scare him off. Rikki's track record with men wasn't exactly stellar. She ended up boring the crap out of them and they eventually walked.

"Surprise me," she said. "I'm not a picky eater. I like just about anything. Since I don't know what restaurants are in town, you'll know better than me what will be good."

"Okay. I guess I'll see you in an hour. I'll bring some tools in case I need them for the computer desk."

"All right."

Torger gave Rikki the same stare he had before that made her legs almost turn to jelly. He held her gaze for a few more seconds, then went to walk around her. He took a deep breath as he did. It made her shiver. She turned as he headed to the apartment door. Once he left, she couldn't hold back a grin that had to be goofy, at best. She did a little happy dance, then brought herself back under control.

Rikki grabbed her car keys off the coffee table. She had a trailer to return. And then she'd get to spend the evening with a man who made her hungry for something more than just food.

* * * *

Once Torger reached the sidewalk, he blew out a breath that border-lined on a growl of need. He was going to cross the street to the coffee shop, but decided he'd better take a little walk to get himself calmed down before he did that. Arousal still pulsed through him, making him edgy. He turned to the left and walked away from the apartment.

Rikki was his mate to his vampire and werewolf sides. He remained in a bit of shock over it. Torger had watched her as she'd taken boxes out of the trailer. He'd first been drawn to her looks. She was pretty in a cute kind of way. Her long, black hair flowed over her shoulders, and she had a curvy body that had him unable to tear his gaze off it. The longer he stared, the more the need to go outside and get a better look at her had come over him. As soon as he'd reached the sidewalk, he'd been taken by the urge to protect her, and his body had come to life.

That alone had told him his vampire side recognized her as his mate. He'd wanted to rush across the street and bury his nose in her hair to see if she was for his werewolf side as well, but he'd held back. As he'd waited, the wind had changed direction, blowing in his face. It'd carried Rikki's scent to him. The urge to mate had slammed into him, making his cock hard in a matter of seconds. That was all he'd needed to know to come to the conclusion that she was completely his.

He was a two-thousand-year-old hybrid who was a true immortal, which meant nothing could kill him, and his mate was mortal. Luckily, his older brother, Brolach, had recently become mated to one, so Torger wasn't completely taken off guard by it. Plus, it didn't surprise him. Being alive as long as he had, he'd met plenty of vampires and werewolves alike, and not one female from those races had ever stirred him to claim her as his mate.

Finally feeling as if he'd gotten himself under control, Torger walked to the end of the block, crossed the street, then headed to the coffee shop where his family waited. There would be, of course, questions since he'd up and left without any explanation. And his sister, Kaisa, his twin, would sense something in him. They had that twin awareness thing going on.

Torger stepped into the coffee shop, and sure enough, Kaisa met his gaze with a questioning look lurking in her eyes. There was no point in avoiding it. He crossed to the booth next to the large front window where his sister sat. He slid onto the bench on the opposite side of her. Cameron, a lone wolf and a friend they considered part of their pack, sat next to Kaisa.

"We saw you helping that woman moving boxes," Kaisa said. "What was that all about?"

He decided being blunt and up front was the best way to answer. Get it all out there. "That was Rikki. She's my mate. To my vampire and werewolf sides."

His sister didn't even blink, only nodded. Cameron's eyes widened as an expression of shock crossed his face for a few seconds.

"A mate?" Cameron asked. "Now, when your asshole vampire relatives could show up at any time and possibly make a mess of things?"

Vampires, who were part of his mother's family, had killed his parents and buried his older brother alive two thousand years ago. To a vampire, one of their kind mating with a werewolf, and bearing a child from that union, was considered an abomination. His parents had fled their homeland, Finland, five thousand years before and had come to this part of the world so they could live in peace. They'd been found in the end. His father had been beheaded while his mother burned. She'd been pregnant at the time with Torger and Kaisa. Being hybrids and true immortals, they'd survived and had been raised by a couple who'd been part of the local native tribe.

Now the vampires had returned, hoping to finish them off. They'd recently killed one who'd attacked and captured Waverly, Brolach's mate, but the others would come. It was only a matter of time.

"It's not as if I went out looking for my mate," Torger

said. "Believe me, I'm just as shocked as you."

Kaisa reached across the table and squeezed his hand. "Well, we have to make sure we watch over Rikki. And it might be best if you can hold off claiming her, especially doing any blood exchanges. That way if one of our vampire relatives happen to come across her, he won't scent you on her. As your mate, she'd be in much greater danger."

That was good advice, but Torger seriously didn't think he'd be able to have that much restraint. At least with his werewolf side he wouldn't. To claim her as his mate, he needed to make love to Rikki quite a few times, and once the bond happened, there would be no going back. Unlike a vampire mate bond, which only needed two blood exchanges to form, he'd have no control over the werewolf one. That side of him would ride him to have sex with her. It'd be a hunger that would be very hard to ignore.

He blew out a breath. "I know it would be, but now that I've found Rikki, staying away isn't going to be an option, nor will it be that easy to hold off claiming her."

"Tell me about it," Cameron said. "Once a mating urge hits a male werewolf, he can only think about claiming his mate. Torger being a hybrid, it might temper it some, but it isn't something he can go around acting as if it isn't there."

"Let's take it as it comes," Torger said. "Rikki's gone to return the trailer she rented, then I'm going back to her apartment with Chinese take-out. I promised I'd put together a new computer desk for her."

"Who's Rikki?" Waverly asked as she came to their booth.

"I wondered that myself," Brolach added as he arrived to stand at his mate's side.

Torger turned his gaze on his older brother and Brolach's mate. Brolach had the same eye and hair color as Torger and Kaisa, and he was just as tall as Torger. The only difference between them was the fact Brolach could at times act the ancient he was. Being buried for two thousand years hadn't made him a modern man. Though with Waverly at his side, his brother was improving.

"Rikki is my mate," Torger said. "She just moved into the apartment above the hardware store across the street."

Waverly smiled. "I'm happy for you, Torger, but having a human mate comes with risks."

And Waverly would know that from firsthand experience. The vampire who'd captured her had torn into her neck, just about draining her dry. Only Brolach doing the second blood exchange had saved her. Not only did it take two to form a mate bond, it also was enough to turn a human. The only difference between a vampire and a hybrid doing the turning was a human became a day walker when the hybrid did it. Other than that, Waverly was now a vampire with the need to drink blood and had fangs. She was immortal as well, but not a true one.

"We were discussing that," Cameron said.

"What's going on? Did I miss something?" Devin, Waverly's brother, asked as he slid onto the bench seat next to Kaisa and put her arm around her shoulders.

Kaisa slid out from Devin's embrace, causing Cameron to move farther into the corner. "Torger found his mate."

Devin smiled at Kaisa. "You two being twins, maybe that means you'll find yours soon too. I have an idea who it could be." He winked at her.

Torger bit back a smile. Ever since Devin had met them, he'd been trying to get Kaisa to go out with him. He knew what they were, but that didn't put him off in the least. Kaisa, on the other hand, so far, wasn't going for it. Torger could understand why, though. When they'd been young, only in their twenties, his sister had fallen for a native hunter in the tribe they'd grown up in. Even though they'd loved each other, he hadn't been a mate for her werewolf side, and he'd refused to allow her to turn him. Kaisa had had only a few years with her hunter before losing him during a buffalo hunt that had gone wrong. She'd sworn from that day on she'd never give her heart to a human male unless he was truly her mate.

Kaisa rolled her eyes at Devin. "I'm sure you do. Are you ever going to give up?"

"Not a chance." He grinned and winked again.

Even though Kaisa tried to keep Devin at arm's length, Torger had a feeling she liked Waverly's brother more than she wanted to admit.

"Now that everyone knows about Rikki, I'm heading out before I'm late meeting her," Torger said as he slid off the bench to stand next to Brolach.

His brother clapped him on the shoulder. "Bring Rikki around soon so we can meet her."

"I will."

After saying goodbye to everyone, Torger headed out of the coffee shop. Once outside, he decided to walk to the town's only Chinese restaurant since it was on the main street as well.

Finding the best way to protect Rikki from his vampire relatives while she had no clue what he was, would be a challenge. Then there would be the struggle to decide how much time he spent with her, along with how far he'd go on the road to claiming her as his mate. On one hand, doing it as fast as he could held merit. He could keep her at his side all the time. On the other, as Kaisa and Cameron had pointed out, it'd put Rikki at greater risk. He was torn. Holding off went against his nature and the instincts that had kicked in as soon as he'd realized she was his female.

As he arrived at the Chinese restaurant, Torger pushed all thoughts of claiming Rikki aside. For now, he'd enjoy his evening with her and use it to get to know her better.

CHAPTER TWO

Rikki turned in the trailer with no problem, then returned to her apartment. She parked her car behind the building in the spot that was reserved for her. There was no back entrance to her place, so she walked around to the front before she went inside by that door. It wasn't secured, but she didn't mind. Lemmon was a small town, after all.

At the top of the stairs, she unlocked her apartment door and then stepped inside. Seeing all the boxes in the living room made her groan. She hated unpacking as much as she hated packing. Rikki looked at the clock that hung on the wall. She'd finished with the trailer faster than she'd expected. There were still forty more minutes before Torger would return.

Since she had time to kill, she decided she might as well put a dent in the unpacking. Rikki moved the bookshelf she'd brought with her in place against an open space along one of the walls in the living room. She took a step back to make sure it was where she wanted it. Once she placed all her books on it, there would be no moving it without taking them off.

She lugged one of the boxes of books to the bookshelf, then set to work. Rikki once more thought she was being silly for keeping all of them. It wasn't as if she'd ever read them again. Even if she really enjoyed a book, she never reread any of them. Maybe one day she'd get rid of them, but today wasn't it. Especially not after packing and moving them.

Rikki became so involved in what she was doing she didn't pay attention to the time. A knock on her apartment door caused her to jump. She glanced at the clock to find that the forty minutes had flown by. She stood from where she kneeled on the floor in front of the bookshelf, then went to let Torger in, who she presumed had knocked.

She opened the door, then stepped back and waved Torger inside. "I smell Chinese food."

He walked into the entranceway and lifted the large bag he carried. "I hope you like it."

Rikki closed the door behind Torger. "I always say you can't go wrong with Chinese. It's one of my favorites."

"Good. Should I put it on the kitchen table?"

"Sure. Go ahead. I haven't unpacked any of my dishes yet so we're going to have to eat out of the containers."

"That's fine. I had them put some chopsticks in with the food. Can you use them?"

"Yes." Rikki followed Torger into the kitchen. He placed the bag onto the table, then took out container after container of food. Once he was finished, it looked as if there was enough to feed four people. She looked at him. "I hope you don't expect me to eat half of that."

Torger chuckled. "No. I figured I'd buy enough so there'd be leftovers. That way you'll have something to eat for lunch tomorrow and won't have to hurry out to the grocery store."

"Thanks. That was thoughtful of you."

They sat at her small table. Rikki took one set of

chopsticks, removed them from the paper wrapping, and then broke them apart. She reached for one take-out container and pulled it toward her. She took a deep breath, savoring the smell of the curried thin fried rice noodle dish. She took a mouthful and moaned.

Torger chuckled. "Is it good?"

Rikki chewed, then swallowed. "The best. Now I know of one great restaurant to order out to."

"Well, it's the only Chinese restaurant in town, so I guess it's a good thing you like the food there."

She laughed. "Yeah, I would guess so."

They ate in silence. Rikki hadn't realized how hungry she'd been until she'd started eating. Now that she thought about it, the last time she'd had a meal was breakfast, and that had only been a cereal bar. It'd been a three-hour drive from Rapid City to Lemmon, and she hadn't stopped to eat again on the road.

Having taken the edge off her hunger, Rikki said, "You know what I do for a living, but I don't know what you do."

Torger swallowed a mouthful of food before he answered. "Well, at present, nothing. My sister, Kaisa, who is also my twin, and I moved to Lemmon a few months ago. Around the same time we found our older brother, Brolach."

"Found him?"

"Yeah. We were separated when Kaisa and I were born. Our parents had died. We knew about him growing up, but we didn't know where he was until recently."

"Oh wow. It's too bad they couldn't have kept the three of you together when you were kids. I know what it's like being in the system."

"System?"

"Yeah, you know, being in foster homes. I grew up in them. My mom had a drug addiction problem, and I was taken from her when I was six months old. I have no idea who my father is, and I'm not sure if my mother did since she never put his name on my birth certificate. She apparently died of an overdose a year after she lost me so I couldn't ask her even if I wanted to find her."

"Kaisa and I were lucky. A couple took us in as if we were their own and raised us. What about you?"

"I wasn't quite that lucky. I was bounced from foster home to foster home. My foster families didn't mistreat me or anything, but I always knew I wasn't their kid. After I finished high school, I managed to get a college scholarship so I could get my BA in English. I've been on my own ever since."

Torger met her gaze. "What about a boyfriend?"

Rikki smiled. "I don't have one of those. When I get one, he usually doesn't hang around very long. I've been told I'm a bore since I am apparently only interested in books."

"There's nothing wrong with that. There was a time when anyone who could read were considered privileged and well-educated while the rest of the masses weren't."

"Very true, but in this day and age, not so much."

"Well, I don't think you're a bore if you like books."

Torger's gaze heated and made Rikki's heart beat a little faster. There was definite interest, and desire, in his eyes. A throbbing ache deep inside her pussy took up residence, demanding she do something about it. She wondered what *he'd* do if she went under the table and got up close and personal to what he had hidden inside his jeans. It was so tempting, she figured she'd better do something before she acted out her little fantasy.

Rikki pushed back her chair and then stood. "Are you finished eating? I am. Maybe we should get started on putting that computer desk together."

She rambled, and more than likely came across as sounding on the rude side. It was something she couldn't stop herself from doing when she became nervous. Not bothering to wait for Torger's answer, Rikki closed the take-out containers and then put them into the fridge.

"I guess I'm done," Torger said with laugher in his voice. "Let's work on that desk of yours."

Rikki led the way into the living room. She told herself to get a grip and not act like such an idiot as she walked to the box with the desk in it. With Torger helping, she managed to get it open and all the pieces taken out. There seemed to be an awful lot for the size of the desk.

She picked up the instructions and quickly skimmed through them. "Well, this looks like a huge pain in the ass. You might regret volunteering to put it together."

"Here, let me see it," Torger said as he reached for what she held.

As Rikki passed the paperwork to Torger, their fingers touched. A shot of awareness surged through her, making thoughts of what he'd be like in bed fill her mind. This time, her pussy throbbed with arousal and wetness pooled deep inside it.

She gave herself a mental shake. She had to stop thinking about sex with Torger. He was there to put her computer desk together. Once he finished that, then she could test the waters.

Torger shook his head. "It's not that bad." He lifted his gaze to hers. "It'll be a little time consuming."

"If you say so. I'll assist when you need an extra pair of hands, but other than that, you'll be the builder."

"Okay," he said with a chuckle.

As Torger set to work on the assembly, Rikki sat on the floor and watched. She found her gaze drawn to his muscular arms. His T-shirt pulled snuggly against his upper body as he reached for pieces of the table. When he tightened a screw, his muscles flexed, which made them even more noticeable. She'd dated guys who'd worked out, but none of them had been as built as Torger.

They spent the next half hour slowly getting the desk

together. As Rikki had predicted, it turned out to be a huge pain. At one point, Torger swore at it as he reread the instructions for the fourth time. The poor guy looked as if he were ready to throw it out the window, and she wouldn't blame him.

Finally, Torger tightened the last screw, then set the desk upright. "Finished. Where would you like it?" he asked as he stood.

Rikki stood as well. "Just up against the wall there will be fine." He shifted it in to place. "Thanks. I think I'm going to owe you something else since you paid for our dinner."

Torger stepped closer and looked into her eyes. "What would you say about paying me back with a kiss?"

She sucked in a sharp breath as her body went into arousal mode. It took everything in her not to throw herself into Torger's arms and devour his mouth. She was that keyed up. Instead, she silently nodded.

*

Torger had done his best to ignore Rikki's enticing scent as he'd worked on assembling her computer desk. It'd been impossible. It filled his nose with every breath he took, going straight to his head. He'd found it hard to concentrate on the task he was doing. His cock was hard and ached. All he wanted to do was drag her into his arms and show his mate what her closeness did to him.

Having Rikki say she owed him something else for the work he'd done, he couldn't pass up the opportunity to ask for a kiss. He wanted, no, needed, that small contact — badly. It'd test the waters to see if she was willing to accept him in that way. Not that the scent of her arousal hadn't already told him that.

At her nod, Torger put his arms around her and tugged her closer until they were chest to chest. The scent of

Rikki's arousal became stronger. Her nipples pebbled beneath her shirt, brushing against him with each rapid breath she took. His erection strained against the front of his jeans. He had to resist the urge to growl with need like the wolf he was. His vampire side wanted to sink its fangs into her neck, preferably while they had sex.

He lowered his head and took her mouth with his. Torger brushed his lips along her plump ones until a soft moan escaped Rikki. That was all the encouragement he needed to deepen the kiss. He increased the pressure as he pushed his tongue inside. It was his turn to moan at the taste of her.

Rikki lifted her hands and placed them on the tops his shoulders as she rubbed against his hard cock. Torger held her tighter, angling his mouth for a better fit along hers. He plunged his tongue in and out like he wanted to do with his shaft inside her pussy.

He shifted his hands from her waist to her bottom. He held it as he ground against her. His blood heated, and the urge to take her rode him hard. Torger picked up Rikki without breaking contact with her lips, then carried her to the couch. He sat on it as he positioned her so she straddled his lap.

She rode his cock through his jeans as she sucked on his tongue. He held her hips, lifting his to match her strokes. He cupped the back of her head and dragged his lips from her mouth to her jawline. He left a line of wet kisses before he reached the side of her neck. His fangs extended at the feel of her rapid pulse beating against his mouth. He couldn't stop himself from dragging the sharp points along her delicate skin. She sucked in a deep breath and quivered.

It took more self-control than he liked not to bite Rikki. Thinking it was best not to see how far he could go without doing it, Torger left her neck and nuzzled between her full breasts as he cupped them. She arched her back, pushing the mounds toward him.

He couldn't hold back a quiet growl. He grabbed the bottom of her shirt and lifted it to her chin. Her bra did up in the front. He undid the clasp, then pushed the cups to the sides, baring her breasts to his sight. Her rosy-pink nipples were taut, begging him to suck on them. Who was he to deny them? He bent his head and swirled his tongue around one tight peak before he sucked it into his mouth.

Torger switched to her other nipple, giving it the same attention. Rikki panted, and her movements grew jerky. His cock throbbed in time with his rapidly beating heart. He could almost feel her moist walls closing around his length as he sank inside her pussy over and over again until they cried out in ecstasy. It'd be so easy to take off their jeans and do what was so vivid in his mind. The only thing holding him back was the fact it'd put them that much closer to his werewolf side claiming her.

He released her nipple and looked up at her. Rikki had her eyes closed and her mouth was slightly open as she breathed at a fast rate. Her checks were flushed with arousal. God, she was beautiful. Torger cupped her face and ran the pad of his thumb along her bottom lip that was swollen from his earlier kisses. She opened her eyes that were filled with desire and met his gaze.

"Why did you stop?" Rikki asked in a husky voice.

"I think we should slow things down a bit. You had a big move today. I bet it wore you out since you did most of it yourself. When I take you to bed, I want you well-rested. There wouldn't be much sleeping going on. Plus, I don't want you to have the idea that I'm only interested in a one-night stand."

Rikki smiled. "You're right. The move is going to catch up with me soon and I'm going to crash." She leaned down and brushed her lips against his before straightening. "I'm glad you don't want only one night. I don't do those. And I'm going to hold you to the no sleeping part."

"We'll wait until you're unpacked and organized. That way you'll have a chance to get to know me better."

"I guess that means I'll be seeing more of you?"

"Of course. Try to get rid of me."

Torger swallowed back a groan of disappointment as Rikki did up her bra and then tugged the front of her T-shirt down. He might not want to have sex with her right then, but he liked looking at her body. He couldn't wait to strip her completely naked and learn every inch of her soft skin with his lips and tongue.

Rikki slid off his lap to sit beside him. "You want to watch some TV with me? The cable is hooked up since it's included in my rent. I'd offer you a beer, but I haven't gone to the store yet so I don't have any."

He put his arm around her shoulders and tucked her against his side. "TV sounds good. And that's fine about the beer."

They watched television for a couple hours before, as Rikki had predicted, she fell asleep with her head on his chest as she snuggled against him. She didn't even wake up when he lifted her into his arms and then carried her to her room. He pulled back the covers on the bed so he could tuck her in.

Torger watched her sleep for a few minutes, then headed to the apartment door. He turned the lock on the knob before he closed it behind him. As he walked down the flight of stairs to the street, he smiled. Having his mate in his arms had felt more than right. He couldn't wait to get her into bed and see how passionate she could be.

CHAPTER THREE

Rikki slowly came awake and stretched. As her hand hit the pillow next to her, she realized she was in her bed. She had no recollection of getting into it. The last thing she remembered she'd been with...

She threw back the covers, sat up and looked down at herself. She wore the same clothes she'd worn yesterday. Crap. She must have fallen asleep on Torger, and he being the nice guy he was, had put her to bed. Rikki was surprised she hadn't woken up when he had. She normally didn't sleep that deeply. The move had to have tired her out more than she'd thought.

Now that she was awake, Rikki figured it would be a good time to have a shower. She slid off the bed, then went in search of the box where she'd packed her towels. She was going to have to make a concerted effort to get everything unpacked today. Even though she'd shared her former place, she'd still had stuff in a storage locker. She'd moved all of it when she came to Lemmon. It'd been a fair amount, even without furniture included. She had to wonder if she had a bit of a hoarder in her.

After finding a towel, her toothbrush, toothpaste, and a comb, Rikki brushed her teeth, then showered. As she dressed, she though that before she got into the unpacking, she should do some grocery shopping. She had the leftover Chinese food for lunch, but nothing to make for dinner.

The one nice thing about living on the main street of a small town was the fact most of the local businesses could be found there. The grocery store was only a block away. She could have walked there, but since she needed to do a big shopping, it'd be easier to drive instead of having to carry all the bags home.

Rikki left her apartment, then went to the back of the building before she got into her car. Less than a minute later, she drove into the parking lot of the grocery store. It'd be considered small for a big city, but it was the only one the town had.

She walked through the store's entrance, then grabbed one of the shopping carts at the front. Rikki headed to the fresh produce section. She hadn't made a list of what she had to buy since she basically needed everything.

She'd reached the end of the produce when she caught a quick glance of a blond-haired man, who she thought could be Torger. He'd been tall enough and had the same build. Rikki hurried after him.

"Torger," she called.

The man turned toward her. He smiled. He definitely wasn't Torger, but he had very similar looks. Plus, now that she really looked at him, his hair was a lot longer.

He came closer. "I think you mistook me for my brother." He smiled again. "I'm Brolach. And I'm thinking you must be Rikki."

Rikki grinned and nodded. "Yes, I am. I take it Torger told you about me."

"He did. I understand you moved to Lemmon yesterday."

"Yes. Torger was nice enough to help lug some of my

boxes up to my apartment."

"He said he had. Since you live across the street from my wife's family's coffee shop, where we work, I expect we'll be seeing each other often."

"The chances are pretty good," Rikki said with a grin. "I've already planned to go there for lunch sometime."

"If you hang around Torger long enough, you'll be going to the shop quite a bit. He, my sister, and our close friend, Cameron, stop by for coffees and donuts almost every day."

"So that's how Torger saw me moving all by myself. He had to have been there."

Brolach smiled. "Yes. I should let you finish your shopping. I look forward to seeing you again, Rikki."

"Thanks. And me too."

Brolach walked away, and Rikki chuckled to herself. Well, that was one way of meeting a family member of a guy she hoped to have a relationship with. And Torger's brother definitely wasn't hard on the eyes.

She continued her shopping, then went to the checkout. Rikki couldn't help but cringe a little when the cashier told her what her total came out to be. At least she was stocked up for a while.

After she loaded the shopping bags into the trunk of her car, she headed to her apartment. As she parked behind the building, she wished there was a back entrance to her place. It would have made it a bit easier to get the groceries upstairs. She ended up making three trips. Her back and legs screamed at her. The move had made her sore and carrying bags up the stairs was just more of the same.

She put the groceries away, then ate some of the Chinese food since it was pretty close to lunchtime. After getting rid of the empty containers, Rikki set to work unpacking dishes, cutlery, glasses, and mugs. She washed each one before putting them into the cupboards and drawers.

Rikki moved on to the living room. She didn't have many things to unpack for that room, except for setting up her work "office," which was basically her desktop computer and printer. Once she did that, she checked her emails.

As usual, getting on the computer led to her doing more than checking if anyone had emailed her. She went to her favorite social media site, and the time slipped away. It was as if she'd blinked and a half an hour had gone by. Rikki forced herself away from her desk and then went to the bedroom to finish the rest of the unpacking. She had a new editing project she should start the next day.

She'd just finished putting the last of the towels and bedding into the linen closet when someone knocked on the apartment door. Rikki went to answer it. After she pulled it open, she smiled. Torger stood on the other side.

"Hi," she said.

"Hi," he replied. "I thought I'd see how the unpacking was going. Plus, Brolach told me he saw you earlier at the grocery store."

"Come on in." Rikki stepped back so Torger could come inside. Once he did, she shut the door behind him. "I finished the unpacking just as you knocked. And yeah, I met Brolach. We didn't talk for very long, but he seemed nice. I have to say good looks run in your family."

Torger put his arms around her and tugged her up against his chest. "I'm glad you think so."

Rikki lifted her face to meet Torger's lips halfway as he claimed hers in a heated kiss. A surge of arousal shot through her as he pushed his tongue inside to duel with her own. No man could make her melt in his arms quite like he did. Aflame with desire, she wanted him to give her sex-starved body exactly what it craved.

*

Torger held Rikki tighter as he deepened their kiss. He'd been waiting most of the day to get her into his arms again. Last night, he'd had several erotic dreams of her. It was his werewolf side making sure he claimed his mate. He woke up feeling a bit on edge and with a raging hard-on.

He lifted his head and looked Rikki in the eyes. "I think we'd better stop here or I'm going to let things get carried away."

She gave him a sexy grin. "Who says we have to stop? I *did* finish my unpacking."

Torger let out a quiet wolf's growl as he reclaimed her lips. There was no way he'd be able to pass up having her when she was willing. The scent of her arousal just ramped up his desire. After dreaming about having her, his body was well-primed.

Rikki clung to Torger as he lifted her off her feet and then carried her down the short hallway to her bedroom. She put her legs around his waist and shoved her hands into the sides of his hair as she enthusiastically kissed him back.

So overtaken with his need to have her, he stopped halfway to the bedroom and put her back against the wall. He ground against her jean-clad pussy as he feasted from her mouth, tasting and sucking. The little moans and groans she made filled his ears and had his cock aching and straining against the front of his pants.

The slight pain of Rikki tugging on his hair had Torger remembering exactly where they were. He didn't want to take her this first time against the wall. It was all right for a quickie, but not what he wanted to do to her right now.

He kept kissing her as he walked the rest of the distance to the bedroom, then crossed to the bed. He placed her onto the mattress and followed her down so he lay stretched out on top of her with his hips wedged between her thighs. The passion that burned between them was hot and quick to flame.

Torger left Rikki's lips and bent his head to nuzzle the side of her neck. His fangs extended, something he had no control over once he was really turned-on. "This is your last chance to say no," he said huskily.

She moaned and rocked her hips against him. "Not going to happen. I have you exactly where I want you."

He dragged a fang across her soft skin, and she shivered beneath him. "Just the answer I wanted to hear."

Torger slid off Rikki to lie at her side. He made sure he kept his mouth closed so she wouldn't see his fangs. He took hold of the bottom of her T-shirt and lifted it off over her head. She undid the front clasp on her bra and removed it before he had a chance to do it. She tossed it over the side of the bed.

He stared at her breasts. Her nipples were taut, beckoning him. Torger bent his head and carefully sucked one into his mouth. He pinched and pulled at the other with his thumb and index finger. Rikki arched her back, pressing closer.

As he sucked, he trailed a hand down her body until he reached the top of her jeans. He undid the button and then opened the zipper. He peeled the material past her hips. She wiggled to help him get them the rest of the way off. He sent her pants in the same direction as her bra.

Torger went up on his hands and knees, straddling Rikki's body. He took her lips in a heated kiss before he worked his way lower to her flat stomach. He swirled his tongue inside her bellybutton before kissing a trail to the top of her panties. He ran a finger just under them. Her belly quivered at his touch.

He hooked the waistband of her panties with his fingers and slid them off her hips before pulling them down her legs to remove them. He ran his gaze over the length of her body, then settled onto the mattress with his shoulders between her spread thighs. The sight of her glistening pussy caused his cock to throb.

Torger dragged a finger through Rikki's wetness, then meeting her gaze, he licked it. Her head fell back as she moaned. She lifted her hips in invitation. He bent his head and swiped her pussy with his tongue. He had to have more.

He set to work pleasuring her with his mouth, lapping and sucking. Torger soon brought a finger into play. He stroked it in and out of her slick opening, then added a second. She moaned his name as she rode them, matching the pace he set. Her inner muscles squeezed them.

He continued to thrust into her as he focused his attention on her clit. Torger flicked it with his tongue, then sucked on the bundle of nerves that was the center of Rikki's pleasure.

Torger would have made Rikki come that way, but she yanked on his hair until he rose above her. "You have too many clothes on," she said huskily. "I want my chance to explore you as you did me." She gave him a kiss, then shoved him onto his back.

He gave her a closed-mouthed smile. "Go ahead. I know it'll be my pleasure."

She grabbed the bottom of his shirt and pulled it up and off. Rikki threw it over her shoulder. "And mine as well."

She ran her gaze over his upper body, and Torger could almost feel as if it were a physical caress. Next, Rikki set to work undoing his jeans before she removed them. He was now as naked as she.

"Commando," she said as she licked her lips. Her gaze landed on his fully erect cock.

"Always," he said in a strained voice. At two thousand years old, he'd never taken to wearing underwear when he'd spent the majority of his life not adding that undergarment to his wardrobe.

"Good to know."

Rikki positioned herself over him and took the same trail down his body that he'd used on hers. She started at his chest and kissed across each pec. At his nipples, she dragged the flat of her tongue along one and then the other. He sucked in a sharp breath.

Torger fisted the sheets to stop himself from pushing Rikki lower to where he ached the most. Unaware, she continued her exploring, using her lips and tongue. She slowly worked her way to his stomach, gently nipping the muscles there.

As she came closer to his straining cock, Torger couldn't hold back a growl. He lifted his head to see what Rikki's reaction was to it, but she didn't seem to notice and kept kissing her way ever lower. He couldn't tear his gaze away.

Another growl escaped him as she reached the place on his body where he wanted her to lavish with attention. She fisted his shaft and pumped her hand up and down his length. She continued the movement until a bead of pre-cum appeared on the very tip. She held him tight at the base and licked the moisture away.

Torger groaned and lifted his hips, unable to stay still any longer. Rikki gave him another lick before she opened her mouth and took his cock inside. She sucked him back as far as she could manage, then slid him almost all the way out. Having his mate suck him off was the most erotic thing he'd ever seen. He grew even harder.

Her head bobbed as she took him in and out, sucking hard and stroking his base. He thrust his hips to match the pace she set. She made him so damn hard. It'd be so easy for her to make him come that way, but he'd stop her before he reached that point. When he did that, he wanted to be buried as deep inside her as he could get.

As if she'd read his mind, Rikki released his cock, then shifted so she straddled his hips. She took hold of his shaft, lined it up with her pussy, then slowly worked him inside. Having her inner muscles embracing him, holding him tight, was the best thing in the world.

Torger watched his cock move in and out of Rikki's pussy as she rode him. She angled her thrusts to put him right where she wanted him. She panted and moaned. He looked up to see she had her eyes closed, and she wore an expression of pleasure. He reached between them and found her clit. He stroked it, hoping to push her over the edge into release.

That did the trick. Rikki's movements became jerky, then she threw back her head and let out a long, whimpered moan. Her inner walls clutched and released his cock as she climaxed. He fought to keep his orgasm at bay, wanting her to have her pleasure first.

Once the spasms ceased, Torger held on to Rikki's hips to keep them joined as he flipped her onto her back. He propped himself up onto his bent arms, then surged in and out of her. She lifted her legs to either side of him, which had him sinking deeper. He grew even harder.

As his climax built, the urge to feed from Rikki took hold. The sound of her rapidly beating heart called to him. His fangs throbbed in time with his dick. He buried his face in the crook of her neck and dragged a sharp point over her skin. He fought to hold back from biting her. That was new for him. Over his long life, he'd had plenty of sex with human women. Not once had he bordered on losing control of his feeding. With his mate, instincts ruled, and they urged him to make the first blood exchange.

Torger thrust faster and harder. He forced himself to lift his upper body onto his straightened arms to avoid temptation. Rikki cried out as she came a second time, which was all he needed to follow her. He growled as his cock pulsed deep inside her with his release.

He collapsed on top her. The need to bite was there still, but not nearly as strong as it'd been before he'd climaxed.

As his shaft softened, he pulled out of her, then rolled to his back. She snuggled up against him with her head pillowed on his chest. He wrapped his arms around her. Neither of his sides had claimed her as mate, but he had a feeling it was only going to be a matter of time. And there wasn't much he could do to stop it.

CHAPTER FOUR

Rikki allowed herself to bask in the moment as Torger held her close. Making love to him had been everything she'd hoped for and more. It was something she didn't regret. How could she when it was the best sex she'd ever had? And she didn't think that way only because she hadn't had any in a while.

She tilted her head and kissed Torger's chin. "That was nice. Really nice, actually."

He ran a caressing hand up and down her back. "It was. I plan to do it again, many times."

"I like the sound of that."

Rikki expected Torger to initiate a second round of lovemaking right then, but he kissed the top of her head before he pulled away and sat up. He swung his legs over the side of the bed.

"Are you going somewhere?" she asked as she sat up behind him.

He looked over his shoulder and smiled. "We both are."

"I thought maybe you wanted to, you know, make love again."

Torger leaned back and gave her a kiss. "Don't worry. We're going to do that. Only it'll have to wait until we come back here."

"Where are we going?"

"I figured we'd go across the street to the coffee shop so you can meet Kaisa and Cameron. They're probably there now. Brolach and Waverly won't be since they have the day off work."

Rikki shifted to sit at Torger's side, then ran her hand up and down his muscular thigh. "Are you sure you want to go this instant? There's plenty of time for me to meet them another day."

He picked up her hand and kissed the tips of her fingers. "True, but I think you should get to know them as soon as possible, especially Kaisa." Torger smiled. "Remember, I said I'd try to break you of your loner ways."

He let go of her, stood, then picked his jeans off the floor. Torger put them on before he grabbed his T-shirt. Rikki really didn't understand why he wanted the meeting to take place now. Obviously, he wouldn't be put off, though.

Rikki slid off the bed and then gathered up her clothes. She headed to the bathroom. After using the toilet, she dressed. She came out to find Torger waiting for her in the hallway.

"All ready to go?" he asked.

She nodded. "Yes, but it's still not too late to change your mind." Rikki gave Torger what she hoped was a sexy grin and not a goofy one.

He chuckled and shook his head. "Come on. You need to meet new people, besides me, that is."

"Fine. We'll go."

Torger grabbed her hand, and then led Rikki out of the apartment. He waited for her to lock the door behind them before they headed down the stairs to the street level. It was just a short walk to arrive at the coffee shop.

He held the door open for her so she could enter ahead of him. There was a good amount of people sitting at tables, and the delicious smell of coffee and donuts made her think it wasn't such a bad idea coming there, after all. She followed him to a booth where a man and woman sat, next to the large front window. The woman had similar enough features for Rikki to presume that she was Kaisa, his sister, which meant the man was Cameron.

Her assumption proved correct when Torger introduced them. Cameron slid out of his side of the booth and then sat next to Kaisa so Rikki and Torger could sit together. A waitress arrived and asked Rikki and Torger what they'd like to order. Rikki settled for a coffee and a Boston cream donut. Torger ordered the same.

"So you must be Torger's new girl," Cameron said. Kaisa gave him a hard stare. He looked back at her. "What? I'm only stating the truth. I can smell him on —"

He didn't get to finish his sentence since Kaisa elbowed him in the stomach, and his breath came out in a loud *whoosh.*

"Never mind him," Kaisa said as she flicked Cameron a hard glance. "He sometimes doesn't know how to be polite."

Rikki chuckled. "It's okay. Really." She looked at Cameron. "And yes, I'm Torger's new girl." He gazed at Kaisa with a smug expression.

"Are the two of you a couple?"

Kaisa gave an exaggerated shudder. "No, thank goodness. Cameron is more a brother to Torger and me. At times, an annoying younger brother."

"Hey," Cameron said with a scowl. "I may not be as ancient as you, but I'm not annoying." Kaisa arched a brow in his direction. "Okay, most of the time I'm not."

Kaisa shook her head. "Whatever helps you sleep at night."

"And this is usually the time when I have to come between the two of them or the taunting gets out of hand," Torger said with a laugh.

Rikki laughed with him. There was no mistaking the closeness between Torger, Kaisa, and Cameron. It was something her life lacked—being part of a family. Having been moved from foster home to foster home as she grew up was a big reason she was such a loner. It was easier to keep distant from people so as not to get her expectations dashed.

Torger put his arm around her shoulders and pulled her against his side. He met her gaze with laughter in his eyes. "If Cameron acts up, you can smack him over the nose with a rolled-up newspaper like a bad puppy."

She looked at Cameron, who shook his head and rolled his eyes.

"Nice," Cameron said. "I'm a pup, am I? At least I'm not an old dog."

Apparently, they liked to use dog references between them when they wanted to make a dig at each other. Rikki found it amusing. As did they.

"Woof, woof," Torger said with a chuckle.

The waitress returned with Rikki's and Torger's coffees and donuts. Once she placed them in front of them, she left. Torger released Rikki, and she took a sip of her coffee. It was good. After a bite of the donut, she let out a sigh of contentment.

"It's good, isn't it?" Cameron asked with a smile. "They have the best donuts. I found this place shortly after I moved here, and I've come every day since. Devin, Waverly's brother, makes all of them."

Rikki nodded. "It is good. Torger told me Waverly's family owned the coffee shop, and that she and Brolach work here."

"It just so happened that was how I found Brolach. Kaisa and Torger had been searching for the older brother they knew they had but hadn't met. They'd gotten a lead that pointed to him being around this part of South Dakota. I came ahead of them, and accidently ran in to Brolach at the shop one day. He'd only been in Lemmon a day. That was a couple months ago. And he and Waverly had just met."

She looked at Torger. "I thought you said Waverly and Brolach were married?"

"They are," he replied.

"Wow, your brother must be a fast worker to have married Waverly after only knowing her a couple months."

"You could say that. I guess when you know you've met the right person there's no point in waiting."

The way Torger looked at her, as if he were talking about her, made Rikki swallow and her heart beat a little faster. Did he really think along those lines after only knowing her for a day? She wasn't one of those people who believed in love at first sight. To be honest, she hadn't had much experience with that emotion.

Rikki broke eye contact with Torger and concentrated on eating her donut and drinking her coffee. He did the same, but as the conversation shifted to other topics, she felt him glancing at her every so often.

Cameron drained the rest of his coffee, then said, "I guess I'm going to head off and do some hunting. Kaisa, you going to join me?"

Torger's sister nodded. "Sure."

"You're hunters?" Rikki asked. "I'm not, but I didn't think there was anything in season yet, not until the fall. That's another month away."

Kaisa and Cameron looked at each other before Torger answered for them. "Cameron didn't mean he was actually going out hunting. He's helping us find relatives on our mother's side of the family. He refers to it as being on the hunt. For information."

"Ah," Rikki said as she nodded. "I gotcha. I guess if I ever wanted to look in to my mother's family, I should talk to Cameron then. Being raised in foster care, I wouldn't even know where to start."

Kaisa pushed Cameron. "Let's go." Her gaze seemed to settle on a man who appeared around Rikki's age, who'd stepped through a door that led to the kitchen. "Now before Devin gets here."

Cameron shook his head and chuckled but did as Kaisa had said. He slid out of the booth so she could as well, then they hurriedly left the coffee shop.

Rikki turned to Torger. "What was that all about?"

He laughed. "Devin likes Kaisa and has been trying to convince her for the last couple months to go out on a date with him. She keeps turning him down."

The man arrived at their table. "Where did Kaisa go?"

"You just missed her, Devin," Torger replied.

"Damn. One day she's going to stop running from me." He looked at Rikki. "You have to be Rikki. I'm Devin, Waverly's brother."

She smiled at him. "Hi. I'm glad I was able to meet you. I have to say you make the best Boston cream donuts I've ever tasted."

Devin grinned. "Thanks. I should head back to the kitchen. I'll see you around, Rikki."

He turned and walked away. "Devin seems nice," Rikki said as she gazed at Torger.

"He is. Don't let Kaisa's behavior fool you. I think she has feelings for Devin. In time, I can see the two of them getting together." He brushed a kiss across her lips. "Shall we get out of here?"

She nodded. "Sure."

Torger dug into his pocket for some money and then left enough on the table to cover their bill and a tip for the waitress. He slid out of the booth and held out his hand to help Rikki, which she accepted.

"Where to now?" she asked once she stood in front of him.

He pulled on her hand so her chest met his. Torger gave her a wickedly sexy grin. "Your place."

A shiver of arousal tore through Rikki. There was no mistaking what would happen once they arrived at her apartment. Already her body readied itself for Torger's. Moisture pooled between her legs, and her nipples had grown taut.

"Let's go. Now," she said.

She turned and tugged him toward the door. He chuckled as he easily kept up with her hurried steps. They raced across the street as if there were a fire. Well, there was one, but it burned deep inside her.

Even though it'd only been an hour or so since they'd last made love, Rikki was desperate to have Torger again. After they stepped through the door, they didn't waste any time going up the flight of stairs. At the top, she dug her keys out of her jeans pocket. Her hands shook as her excitement grew. It took her a couple tries to get the key into the lock. Once she unlocked it, she pushed opened the apartment door and then quickly found herself wrapped in his embrace.

Torger kicked the door shut before he walked them into the living room. They tore at each other's clothes. There would be no making it to the bedroom this time. Not that Rikki cared. The floor, or even the couch, would be just as good as her bed. As long as they had a surface for them to get down and dirty on, she didn't care. She wanted him inside her right there, right now.

Once they were naked, they fell into each other's arms, and ended up on the carpeted floor with Torger on top of Rikki. His hard cock brushed against her wet pussy as his hips settled between her spread thighs. She lifted hers at the right angle, and the head of his shaft slipped inside her.

They both moaned. After Torger worked his entire length as deep as it would go, he reached under her to cup her bottom, then pistoned in and out. He took her in slow, hard thrusts. She squeezed her inner muscles around his plunging cock. He made that growling sound he'd used the first time they'd been together like this. There was also the sensation of a sharp tooth being dragged against the side of her neck. Neither of those things put a damper on her arousal. They actually increased it.

Rikki held on to Torger's shoulders and matched the pace he set. He surged into her faster, and the sounds of pleasure he made increased in volume. She moaned right along with him, lost in the pleasurable sensations that washed through her.

It was as her climax edged ever nearer to the surface did she feel something else stirring. It was a new sensation. The best way she could describe it was if a piece of Torger's soul reached out for a piece of hers. It made her gasp as the two brushed against each other, then became one.

As if that were the on switch to her orgasm, it tore through her like a freight train, and was just as unstoppable. It was intense and seemed to go on and on. Torger's cock pulsed deep inside her pussy as he came. During it, there was a sharp pain in her neck as if he'd bit her. She was thrown into another release and found herself on the verge of passing out as a sense of ecstasy swamped her.

*

Torger couldn't help himself. He sank his fangs into Rikki's neck as they came and drank. Having his werewolf side claim her, form the bond that joined their souls, had made his control slip. And the taste of her blood, God, it was unlike anything he'd had before. All the donors he'd used over the long years couldn't compare to his mate's sweetness.

As she sighed and grew limp, he quickly realized he'd taken too much blood. He hadn't wanted to do it, but he'd put Rikki at risk. Torger licked his bite mark on her neck to seal and heal the wound before he brought the inside of his wrist to his mouth and bit.

Once his blood rose to the surface, he placed his arm against her lips. "Drink, Rikki."

She was barely aware of what he did, but she closed her mouth on his wrist and drank. It only lasted a few seconds, but it was enough to restore what he'd taken and to complete the first blood exchange. They were now well and truly on the road to his vampire side claiming her as his werewolf one had. There was no going back.

Rikki sighed again, then fell into a deep sleep. Torger pulled out of her before he scooped her up into his arms. Once inside her bedroom, he tucked her into bed. He looked down at her. He loved her. He had from the moment he'd realized what she was to him.

He went back into the living room and gathered up their strewn clothes. He smiled. They really had been impatient to have not even made it to the bed. He returned to the other room, then put their clothing on top the dresser before he slipped under the covers next to his mate. He wasn't tired, but he wasn't going to pass up the opportunity to watch her sleep.

Torger pulled Rikki into his arms so she lay against his side. He kissed the top of her head. He was going to tell her everything about his world before he took that final step to bring her fully into it. With the second blood exchange, she'd be fully turned into a vampire. She'd no longer be able to eat food. She'd subsist on his blood. Unlike other vamps, she'd be a day walker, and would be able to move freely while the sun was out.

Once she awoke from her sleep, he promised himself

he'd tell her the truth of what he was. Hopefully, she wouldn't fear him afterward. When Brolach had found Waverly, he'd had to compel her not to be afraid. Torger didn't want to resort to that unless it was absolutely necessary. Using compulsion on his mate wasn't exactly something he should be doing to the woman he loved.

CHAPTER FIVE

Rikki came awake and looked around, not sure where she was at first. Then it hit her that she was in the bedroom in her new apartment. She looked at the window. It was still light out, but it wasn't as bright as it had been before she'd fallen asleep. The clock on her bedside table showed it was early in the evening. Since it was edging near fall, it'd be getting dark soon.

"Shit," she said as she threw back the covers.

It didn't take her long to realize she was naked. It all came rushing back to her. She and Torger had made love in the living room after returning from the coffee shop. She must have fallen asleep right after. That was twice now he'd put her to bed.

Rikki hoped Torger hadn't left. As she spotted her clothes piled on top her dresser and went to get them, she sniffed something delicious coming from the other side of the closed bedroom door. Was he cooking them dinner?

She dressed, then hurried out to the kitchen. Torger stood before the stove, stirring something in a pot. He was dressed as well. He turned his head and smiled as she came closer.

"How long was I asleep?" she asked, then gave him a quick kiss on the lips.

"A couple hours."

"Why did you let me sleep for so long?"

He smiled. "You obviously were tired and needed the rest. I didn't mind. I actually climbed into bed and held you for a while before I got up. I was getting hungry, and I figured you'd be once you were awake, so I decided to cook us something."

"What are you making? It smells really good."

"Baked herbed chicken breasts, fettuccini alfredo, and steamed broccoli."

"I don't think when I went shopping this morning I bought the ingredients to make all that."

Torger chuckled. "You didn't. I made a run to the grocery store while you were sleeping. I borrowed your keys so I could lock the door and not have to wake you up to let me back in. I hope you don't mind."

"Of course not."

"Good. Dinner is almost ready. Why don't you set the table while I finish up?"

"I can do that."

Rikki went to the cupboard and took out two dinner plates. She placed those on the table before she went for the cutlery. By the time she was finished arranging the place settings, Torger had everything done. He dished up while she took a seat.

She hadn't realized how hungry she was until she had her first mouthful of food. It was delicious. The alfredo sauce was made from scratch, and in no way compared to the noodle packages she usually bought.

"How is it?" Torger asked.

"Really, really good. How would you like the job of being my personal chef? There are times when I get so deep into editing I forget to eat. And when I do cook, I'm nowhere near as good as you."

He smiled. "Well, thanks. I'll have to keep that job offer in mind."

They continued eating, and Rikki seriously thought up ideas on how to work it so Torger would cook for her more often. She was more than willing to pay him with sex. She'd have a good meal, then get the best dessert ever — his hot bod. Maybe he'd let her put whipped cream on him and then lick it off. That way he'd truly be a dessert.

The sound of a cell going off broke Rikki out of her thoughts. Torger put down his fork before he took his phone out of his front jeans pocket. He looked at the screen, then answered the call.

"Hey, Cameron. What's up?" His smile slipped away to be replaced by a stern expression. "Where are you?" Torger remained silent as Cameron answered on the other end. "You and Kaisa stay where you are. I'll be there in a few minutes." He disconnected the call.

"Is everything okay?" Rikki asked.

"Something has come up. I have to meet with Kaisa and Cameron. I don't know if I'll be able to come back later."

"Don't worry about it. If your sister and friend need you, then go. We can always see each other tomorrow. It isn't as if you don't know where I live."

Torger leaned toward her and gave her a short, thorough kiss. "Thanks for being understanding. And sorry for sticking you with all the dirty dishes."

"Hey, you cooked. It's only fair I should do the washing up. Go."

He stood, then went to the apartment door. Torger turned and blew her a kiss before he walked out. Rikki smiled. He was cute.

She collected their dirty dishes, then put them into the dishwasher. She filled the sinks to wash the pots and pans that Torger had used to cook their meal. Her thoughts gravitated toward him. So far, he came across as being perfect. The man cooked. She only hoped he wouldn't be too good to be true. She hated that the thought had even crossed her mind, but the way she'd grown up, she found it hard to trust what a person actually was at face value. Rikki had learned that lesson the hard way with a few foster parents. At first, they'd come across as great people, who only wanted the best for her. After a few months, they'd made it perfectly clear they were in it just for the money.

Rikki was halfway done washing the dishes when someone knocked on the apartment door. She dried her hands on the tea towel that she had over her shoulder before she put it on the table. She smiled as she crossed to the entrance. Maybe it was Torger, finished up with whatever he had to do with Cameron and Kaisa.

She opened the door, about ready to say he'd been quick. Rikki stopped herself as her gaze landed on the man who stood on the other side. It wasn't someone she'd met. The first thing she noticed was that he wasn't bad looking, but his skin was so pale it was as if he'd never been out in the sun. Like ever.

"Can I help you?" she asked.

He dragged in a deep breath through his nose, then gave her a wide smile that gave her a good view of what she could only describe as fangs. The kind vampires in the movies and on TV had.

"It would seem as though you can, even better than I'd expected," he said as he grabbed her by the throat and walked her backward farther into the apartment.

Rikki wanted to scream, but he tightened his grip, cutting off most of her airway. She clawed at his hand and fought to breathe. She was on the verge of passing out when he allowed her to drag in a lungful of air.

"No screaming," he said. He lowered his head so their gazes met. "Look into my eyes." She did and felt as if she fell into a dazed state. His voice washed over her as if he were far away, but it seemed to resonate deep inside her. "You will do everything I say, then forget I was ever here."

Rikki blinked and found herself standing in front of the sink, staring at nothing. She gave herself a mental shake. Man, she had to have it bad for Torger to get so lost in thoughts of him that she forgot what she was doing. She dipped her hand into the wash water and found it'd cooled. She really had been off in another world. She ran the hot water to warm what was in the sink, then continued with the chore at hand.

* * * *

Torger got out of his car, then walked to where Kaisa and Cameron stood, waiting for him. They were not too far from Lemmon's grain elevator, which was situated close to the train tracks near the outskirts of town. Since it was past business hours, the place was deserted.

"So, what happened?" Torger asked as he came to stand in front of them.

Kaisa answered. "Cameron tracked down the scent of a servant. It was the weirdest thing. Once we caught up to him, he stood out in the open as if he wanted us to find him."

A servant was a human a vampire compelled to do their bidding without question, and to put the needs of their master before their own. Even if it meant they had to give up their lives to serve him or her. Not all vamps had them. Only the ones who were evil at heart.

"What did this servant want?" Torger asked.

"To give us a message. He said his master would be here in Lemmon soon, and would come hunting us. And that they know we killed his master's cousin. Apparently, we'll pay for that with our lives."

Torger snorted. That sounded in character with the vamps in his mother's family. They were arrogant to a fault, and thought they were all-powerful. The thought that he, Brolach, and Kaisa were all true immortals, unable to be killed, wouldn't have even crossed their minds.

"Did you call Brolach and tell him what the servant said?" he asked.

Cameron nodded. "I did. He'll be extra observant whenever he and Waverly are out or at the coffee shop, working. Not that a vampire would show up there then since they work dayshift."

No, one wouldn't, but a human servant could. The vamp they'd killed had had two of them, who'd captured Waverly during the day. That abduction had led to Brolach doing the second blood exchange to claim and turn her to save her life when the vamp had torn into her throat.

Torger nodded. "Brolach is just being cautious of his mate. Something I'll now have to do with Rikki." He met Cameron's and Kaisa's gazes with his own. "My werewolf side has claimed her as mine."

His sister shook her head. "Damn. Why couldn't it have taken longer? What about blood exchanges? Please tell me you didn't do one?"

"Well, it didn't. And I wish I could tell you I didn't, but I can't. Not expecting the werewolf mate bond to form so quickly, I lost control and fed from Rikki. I took too much and had to give her some of my blood."

"So if a vamp happens to come across her, he or she will know you've almost claimed her. That's so not good with one of our vampire relatives on his way here. Did Rikki know what happened?"

"No. She was on the verge of passing out. I acted quickly and then she fell asleep for a few hours. If she remembered any of it—our souls joining or me getting her to drink my blood—she didn't let on."

"You'll have to tell her, brother."

Torger sighed. "I know. Especially now. It might be better if I turn her as soon as possible. That way she'll be immortal and will have a fighting chance if a vampire tries to use her to get to me as the other did to Brolach. Waverly almost died because Brolach had held off the second blood exchange."

Cameron nodded. "I think that'd be best. Until then Rikki will be a vulnerable mortal."

"I'll tell her everything tomorrow. Where's the servant now?"

Cameron blew out a breath. "In the trunk of my car. Right after he delivered his message, he took out a knife and stabbed himself in the heart before we could stop him. I'm going to ditch the body some place where it won't be found. You can drive Kaisa home while I do that."

"Shit," Torger said. "Take care of it. Kaisa, let's go."

They only way to sever a servant's tie to his or her master vampire was to kill the vamp. Even though it sucked that the servant had been ordered to kill himself, in the long run it was for the best.

"Aren't you going to go back to Rikki's place?" his sister asked.

"Not tonight. If I'm going to reveal what I am to her and tell her what it entails to be my mate, I think I'd better work out a plan that won't involve her freaking out. I don't think springing it on her right out of the blue is going to do me any favors. I don't want to use compulsion on her."

"That's probably a good idea. You don't want to lose her trust. And once you turn her, you won't be able to compel her any longer."

Cameron waved and said he'd get home to the house they all shared as fast as he could, then got into his car before he drove off. He headed down the road that would take him farther away from the main part of town. Torger didn't even want to know where Cameron would bury the body of the servant.

He and Kaisa climbed into his car, then he started the

engine. As he drove them home, he tried not to let his worry for his mate's safety take over him. His instincts would blow it all out of proportion before it reached the stage where she was in true danger. After tomorrow, he wouldn't have as much to fear. She'd be his mate in all ways, and he wouldn't leave her side.

CHAPTER SIx

It was the following day, and Torger stood outside the coffee shop with Brolach, Waverly, Kaisa, and Cameron. He was about to cross the street to see Rikki. He'd had a coffee with his family beforehand, and they'd insisted on following him out.

He looked at each one of them. "Are all of you going to hang out here while I'm with Rikki?"

"We just want to be ready in case you need help with telling Rikki the truth," Waverly said. "I know from firsthand experience how hard it can be to accept it all when you think it's only stuff of make believe."

"I think I can handle it on my own."

"Still," Brolach said, "you might appreciate it if it blows up in your face."

"Don't you two have to work?" He set his gaze on Waverly. "Your dad will come looking for you and Brolach."

She waved his concerns away with a flick of her hand. "Dad won't be a problem. Devin said he'd cover for us. And it isn't as if my father is a harsh task master, anyway."

Torger turned his attention on Cameron and Kaisa. "There isn't anything I can say that will send you away either." He said it as a statement, knowing full well there was no point saying it as a question.

His sister smiled. "You have that right."

He shook his head. "Fine. Just so you know, I have no idea how long it'll take me to figure it's the right time to tell her. You all could be standing out here for hours."

Cameron shook his head. "Just get it over and done with. Why prolong the agony?"

"I guess you're right. I'll let you know once it's done."

"We won't come to your rescue unless we hear screaming."

Torger rolled his eyes, then walked across the street. He opened the door to the entrance stairway to Rikki's apartment before he climbed the steps. He took a deep breath. Cameron was correct. There was no sense in waiting for the opportune moment to tell Rikki. It might never come. It was best to get through it as soon as possible so he could put it behind him.

He knocked on the apartment door. His sensitive hearing easily picked up the sound of Rikki moving around on the other side. She opened it, then stepped back for him to enter. Once she closed it behind him, he gathered her into his arms and gave her a long kiss. They were both breathing hard once he let her up for air.

"I missed you," he said.

She smiled. "I can tell. I missed you too."

Rikki took hold of Torger's hand and pulled him to stand in the middle of the living room. He went to embrace her once more, but she stepped out of reach and shook her head with a grin.

"I want you to wait right here," she said. "I have a surprise for you. I have to get it."

"And where exactly is this surprise?"

"In my bedroom."

"Wouldn't it be better if I went with you? I can think of lots of things I can do in that room to show you how much I like the surprise."

"Oh no, you don't. You stay there. I'll be back in a few seconds."

"Fine. You win. I'll wait for you to bring the surprise to me."

Rikki turned and walked toward her room. Torger watched her, wondering what she'd bring back. He was disappointed in himself at how fast he'd latched on to this small diversion from having to tell her his big secret. He wasn't exactly chicken about doing it. He thought his reluctance stemmed from the fact she'd be the first human he'd told.

She returned to the living room with a big smile as she held something behind her back. "Are you ready for your surprise?"

"Yes."

"Good."

Before Torger realized it was a gun Rikki pulled from behind her back, she'd fired. She was close enough not to miss. The bullet hit him smack in the middle of his forehead. He collapsed to the floor like a ton of bricks.

*

Rikki jerked as what sounded like a gunshot rang in her ears. She blinked, not knowing what happened. It was almost as if she'd been sleep walking and then had suddenly woken up.

She looked down at the weight in her hand. She held a gun. Had she fired it? Rikki frantically gazed around the room and found Torger on the living room floor with a bullet wound in the middle of his forehead. He didn't seem to be moving.

Her chest heaved as she breathed at too fast a rate. She

couldn't have shot him. She didn't even own a gun and had no idea where this one had come from or why she'd used it. She hated them.

The sound of the apartment door slamming against the wall drew her gaze. Brolach, Cameron, and Kaisa raced inside. A woman she didn't know followed them. Rikki whimpered and dropped the gun.

As Kaisa rushed to Torger's side, Rikki said on the verge of tears, "I shot him, but I don't remember doing it. I don't remember."

"It's okay, Rikki," Kaisa said.

"No, it's not. I shot Torger. I killed him!" she shouted. "Why can't I remember? Why would I do that? I have deep feelings for him. Why would I kill him?" Her voice rose with each word she spoke.

Kaisa looked at Brolach. "She's getting hysterical."

He nodded. "I'll take care of it."

Brolach crossed to Rikki and took hold of her chin to force her to gaze into his eyes. She felt as if she couldn't break the connection, and that she was in a bit of a daze.

"You're going to be calm. And you're going to remain calm when Torger tells you what we are. You won't fear us — ever."

Once Brolach let her go, Rikki felt calm, just as he'd said she would. What had he done to her?

The woman Rikki hadn't met before came to stand beside Brolach. "I'm Waverly, by the way." She looked at her husband. "Torger is going to be pissed that you compelled his mate. It worked for me when I found you, but I'm yours, and it was your decision, not your brother's."

Brolach shrugged. "He'll thank me for it in the end."

Rikki said calmly, "Torger is dead. I shot him."

Brolach shook his head. "He isn't. See for yourself."

She walked around him and Waverly and then went to Kaisa and Cameron, who were still with Torger. Rikki kneeled at Torger's side. At first, all she could stare at was the bullet wound, but the longer she looked, the blood stopped seeping. She sucked in a sharp breath as the bullet pushed itself out of the wound, which then healed within seconds as if it'd never been there.

Torger groaned. "That smart," he said as he reached up and rubbed his forehead. "Being shot in the head is added to the list of things I don't want to experience again."

"Torger?" Rikki asked in a shaky voice.

He met her gaze and sat up. "I'm okay."

"I'm so, so sorry. I don't know what came over me. Nor where the gun came from. I don't own one, and never have. I don't remember even doing it. I only put it together when I seemed to wake up as if I were sleep walking and found the gun in my hand."

"Shh," he said. "It's all right." He pulled her onto his lap and kissed her. He looked at Kaisa. "She was compelled."

His sister nodded. "Yes. The vampire must already be here. I have a feeling that servant last night was a distraction to get you away from Rikki. The vamp came and used compulsion to get her to shoot you the next time you came to her apartment."

"We have to take him out."

"I know."

"And, ah, why is Rikki so calm?"

Kaisa shook her head. "It wasn't me. Brolach did it. She was hyperventilating and getting hysterical. Being the ancient male that he is, our big brother decided to take matters into his own hands."

Rikki cleared her throat to get their attention. "Can someone please explain what the hell is going on? I should be freaking out right now, but I can't do that even if my life depended on it."

Torger tucked some of her hair behind her ear. "I was going to explain today, but this wasn't how I expected the conversation to come up." He took a deep breath. "Brolach, Kaisa, and I are hybrids, which means our mother was a vampire and our father a werewolf. Cameron is a werewolf. And Waverly, who is Brolach's mate as you are mine, is now a vampire, but a day walker."

Strangely, Rikki didn't feel anything remotely like she should at hearing all that. There was no disbelief, and no fear from knowing it had to be the truth. And it had to be since she'd seen Torger survive and heal from an almost point-blank gunshot wound to the head. No average person could live through it.

"Okay," she said. "First of all, why do I feel so calm? Is it because Brolach told me to be like this?"

Torger shot his brother a dirty look before he met her gaze again and replied, "Yes. Vampires are able to compel humans. When you were getting too upset, Brolach decided to use compulsion to stop you."

"You said I was compelled to shoot you by another vampire. Why don't I remember that?"

"He must have made it so you wouldn't. After I left you last night, at some point, he must have come to the apartment, compelled you, gave you the gun and then left you with no knowledge of it taking place. We had no idea a vampire was here in Lemmon or I wouldn't have left your side."

Being compelled to do anything a vampire wanted was a scary thing. "How can I stop it from happening again? I don't like the feeling of being so vulnerable."

Torger gave Rikki a small smile. "There is one way — we do a second blood exchange, which will turn you into a vampire, a day walker like Waverly. A vamp can't compel another of his or her kind."

She took a deep breath. "So, I'd have to drink blood afterward?"

"Yes. Only mine. You've already had some of it when

we made love the second time. My werewolf side claimed you, and I ended up biting you and taking too much of your blood. I gave you mine to counteract that."

Rikki nodded. "I remember...something...different happening while we, you know. I thought it felt as if our souls joined."

He ran a caressing hand along her cheek. "They did. That was when I claimed you as my mate as a werewolf."

"I want to see your fangs and furry side."

Cameron laughed. "I think this should be our cue to leave. I don't want to be around if Rikki next asks Torger to strip."

Kaisa shook her head. "You mean before you go wolf and get Rikki to pet you. You love being petted."

Cameron scowled. "That's a low blow."

Kaisa and Cameron stood, then joined Brolach and Waverly. "You know where we'll be," Brolach said as they all left the apartment, and then he closed the door behind them.

"I really do want to see your fangs and wolf," Rikki said.

Torger chuckled. "All right."

He opened his mouth, and she saw his fangs. As she watched, they lengthened, then returned to their smaller size. Torger slid her off his lap to sit on the floor before he inched a little away. His body blurred, and then a wolf with fur a shade darker than his blond hair took his place. It sat on its haunches and stared at her. It was huge, much larger than a normal wolf.

Rikki reached out and ran her hand down his back. The jade-green eyes that looked at her were definitely Torger's. Plus, there was no mistaking the intelligence in them.

"Do you understand me?" she asked as she continued to pet him.

His large lupine head moved up and down in an exaggerated nod.

"And you can't talk to me like this?"

Again, Torger the wolf nodded. His body blurred, and he was back to being human. He tugged her into his arms. "I know this is fast, but I love you, Rikki. You have to believe that. You are my mate. I've waited two thousand years to find you. Will you let me do the second blood exchange and turn you? That way you'll be immortal, and I'll feel better when you aren't as vulnerable as you are now."

"You're two thousand years old?"

"Yes. So is Kaisa since she's my twin. Brolach is five thousand."

"I think the subject of your age will be a discussion for another time." Rikki met his gaze. "I really haven't had someone love me before. To be honest, I wasn't sure if I'd recognize it when the time came, or if I was capable of it. Seeing you lying on the floor, while I thought you were dead, I realized I did, and that I actually felt that emotion for you. I've been alone for so long. When I was young, all I ever really wanted was a family. With you, I'll have that. Forever. So, Torger, yes, you can do the second blood exchange."

He cupped her face in his hands. "Are you sure? There's no going back once it's done. You will turn."

"I'm sure." She smiled. "I really think you're going to have to thank Brolach for compelling me to stay calm about all this. I'm finding it really easy to accept everything and want everything that goes with it."

He kissed her long and hard, then stood with her in his arms. Torger carried her to her bedroom and then placed her on the center of her bed. She wrapped him in her embrace as he followed her down.

"You always seem to be carrying me to my bedroom," Rikki said between kisses.

"It gets us there faster."

"I'm not complaining."

He took her mouth again, then stripped them of their clothes. She reached between them and fisted his cock, which was already hard. Being with him like that felt right and had from the very start. Obviously, there was such a thing as soul mates, after all.

He licked and kissed his way from her lips down to her chest. Torger gently dragged a fang across one of her nipples before he took it into his mouth. He sucked on it, then switched to the other taut bud until he had her squirming beneath him. She stroked him, bringing a soft growl out of him.

"Torger," she said on a pant. "I want you inside me."

"Yes," he replied with another growl and a moan.

The head of his cock pushed inside her pussy. She angled her hips to meet his thrusts as he sank deeper and deeper, stretching and filling her. He took her in slow, hard strokes that drove her crazy. She lifted her legs and held on to his shoulders. Having him moving in her was the best feeling ever.

Torger lifted his head and met her gaze. "Once you start to come, I'm going to bite you. That will make me come as well. After that, you can drink from me to complete the second blood exchange."

"Do it."

He groaned as she tightened her inner muscles around his plunging cock.

He lowered his head to the crook of her neck but supported his upper body on his bent arms. He thrust faster, and her release inched nearer to the surface. Just as her orgasm tore through her, he sank his fangs into her neck. She let out a loud, whimpered moan as she was flooded with intense pleasure. He growled, his shaft pulsing deep inside her pussy as he too came.

After the sensations faded, Torger licked where he'd bitten her, then rolled them to their sides. He held her gaze as he brought his inner wrist to his mouth and sank his fangs into his skin. Blood welled when he offered it to her.

Rikki placed her mouth on the bite mark and drank. She'd taken a couple swallows before Torger pulled his wrist away. He watched her intently as he licked it, which healed the small wound.

It only took a few seconds after that for Rikki to start to feel something building inside her. It didn't exactly hurt, but it wasn't comfortable. She grabbed on to Torger's arm as she breathed faster.

"It's okay, Rikki," he said. "It won't last long. I promise."

Along with the almost painful sensation, her gums and eyeteeth burned. She licked each one and found they were sharper and shaped like fangs. By increments, the uncomfortableness eased, and she relaxed. Seconds later, it disappeared altogether.

"How do you feel?" Torger asked.

Rikki took stock of herself. She felt great. Better than great, actually. Her senses seemed more acute. She could hear Torger's heart beating without having to have her ear pressed to his chest. When she concentrated, she even heard his blood surging through his veins. It caused her to hunger for it, and she had to swallow as her mouth watered.

Torger smiled. "I know what you need." He pulled her on top him as he rolled to his back, then turned his head to the side. "My mate needs to feed. Sink your fangs into me."

Rikki didn't hesitate. The urge wasn't something she wanted to ignore. As she bit and drank, Torger's cock hardened between them. She angled her hips just right and took it inside her pussy. She rode her mate as his blood filled her mouth. Once she'd gotten her fill, she licked her bite mark as he'd done to heal it.

She sat up and rode his shaft up and down. Their loud moans and groans filled the room. Rikki was surprised by how close her release was to taking her over. Torger surged upright, sank his fangs into her neck and that was all she needed to climax. He licked her skin, threw back his head on a howl, then gave her everything he had.

As they fought to catch their breaths, Rikki said, "I love you, Torger."

"I love you too."

"I think I'm going to like having fangs. Especially since I get to bite you with them."

"We're not going to be leaving this bed any time soon, are we?" he asked with a laugh.

"No. I think I need some tutoring when it comes to the whole vampire thing. I can't think of a better way to learn than being naked and in your arms."

Torger held her tight as he took her down onto her back with him on top her. "I couldn't agree more."

Epilogue

It'd been a week since Rikki had accepted Torger for what he was and fully became his mate. He'd moved in with her, leaving his sister and Cameron to share the house. For now, his mate's apartment was perfect for them.

The next night after Torger had turned Rikki, he, Cameron, and Kaisa had gone on the hunt for the vampire who'd compelled his mate. They'd searched during the day to see if they could find any servants but had come up with nothing. The vampire hunt had turned out to be the same. Either the vamp had left Lemmon, or he'd found a lair they couldn't find.

Torger had a feeling the bastard was still around. And that the vampire waited either to strike again or for reinforcements. There had been five of them, all related to his mother, who'd taken part in the killing of his mother and father that day of his and Kaisa's birth two thousand years ago. A couple months ago, he and his family had killed one of them. So there were four still to go.

And they would come for him and his family. More than likely very soon. Those perceived high and mighty vampires wouldn't be able to abide hybrid abominations like he, Brolach, and Kaisa to exist for much longer. Not that they could do anything to end their lives. They were true immortals, after all.

Torger leaned back on the couch and looked at Rikki, who sat in front of her desktop computer, editing a book. He smiled. She'd quickly adjusted to being a vampire very well. She no longer needed to consume food but was quite happy to drink from him. They both were.

Becoming mated was the best thing that had ever happened to him. Somehow, he needed to find a human mate for his sister. Kaisa would have none of it, but he was sure she'd be just as happy as he with the final outcome. She only needed a nudge in the right direction.

Rikki pushed the keyboard tray under her desk, then turned her office chair so she faced him. "That's enough for now." She met his gaze. "I'm hungry."

Torger's cock went instantly hard. He stood, then crossed the room with werewolf speed. He yanked his T-shirt off over his head, then bent his head to the side. "Then eat."

His mate threw herself into his arms, taking him down to the floor. Torger gladly lay there as she had her way with him, then sank her fangs into his neck. Yeah, immortal life didn't get much better than that.

The End

TO WIN A HYBRID

Kaisa has a rule about dating male humans. She doesn't. A past relationship had left her unable to trust one again. Then Devin comes into her life and makes her long for things she knows she's better off not feeling. She tries her damned to push him away, but no matter what she does, he won't let her.

Devin wanted Kaisa to be his since the day he'd met her. He has no problem with her being a hybrid, half werewolf and half vampire. In fact, he wants her to turn him, if only to prove he's her perfect mate.

As the vampires who have hunted Kaisa and her brothers for centuries make a move against them, she has to make a decision. Accept Devin into her life or cut him out of it for his own good.

CHAPTER ONE

Devin stood at the kitchen door that led to the main part of his family's coffee shop in Lemmon, South Dakota, and looked out the small window. His gaze unerringly landed on one of the booths that lined the front of the place. Four people sat at it, but he only had eyes for one of them. Kaisa. She flicked her long, blonde hair over a shoulder as she laughed at something said to her. Her laughter reached her jade-green eyes. God, she was gorgeous.

"You know, staring at her like a lovesick puppy dog isn't going to make her more inclined to go out on a date with you."

He turned to find his sister, Waverly, standing behind him. "I know. Can't you put in a good word for me? She's your sister-in-law, after all."

Waverly was mated to Brolach, an ancient hybrid who was half vampire and half werewolf. Kaisa was Brolach's sister, also a hybrid. She and her twin brother, Torger, were two thousand years old. Their older brother was five thousand.

"You know that won't work, Devin." Waverly smiled, flashing him a bit of fang. "Kaisa knows you're a player. Plus, she doesn't want a relationship with a human."

"I might have been one in the past, but not now. And me being human is easy to fix. Kaisa just has to turn me as Brolach did you and Torger did Rikki."

Waverly—thanks to two blood exchanges with Brolach—had been turned into a day-walker vampire. She was basically immortal. Since her mate was a hybrid, he was a true immortal, which meant nothing could kill him, and he would never die.

"Rikki and I are Brolach's and Torger's mates. Turning us was part of them claiming us. You are not Kaisa's mate."

Devin scowled. "You don't know that for sure. I could be. Just because Kaisa is female and unable to have her werewolf or vampire sides sense her mate doesn't mean I'm not the one meant for her. She could turn me and then I'd be able to sense she's mine."

"Not going to happen, big brother. I think it's time for you to admit defeat and move on to someone new."

Waverly walked around Devin, pushed open the kitchen door and stepped into the other part of the coffee shop. He turned toward the window and brought his gaze to Kaisa once again. He hadn't been able to stop thinking about her or trying to get her to go out with him, since she'd walked into his life a few months before. His sister had no idea how bad he had it.

Devin decided it was time for him to take a break when the other cook came through the back door after going outside for a smoke. With a nod to his co-worker, he walked out the kitchen door.

He headed straight for the booth where Kaisa sat. Cameron, the lone wolf who had formed a pack of three with Kaisa and Torger many years ago, noticed him first.

"Have you come for your daily dose of rejection?"

Cameron asked with a grin.

Devin ignored his question. "I want your seat." Cameron sat next to Kaisa.

"What will you give me for it?"

"A free donut." The werewolf loved the coffee shop donuts, which Devin made. Cameron had started the daily ritual of coming there for the sweet pastry and a cup of coffee before Kaisa and Torger had arrived in Lemmon.

Cameron shook his head. "Not good enough."

There was no mistaking the laughter in the other man's eyes. Devin blew out a breath. "All right. How about a free dozen donuts for you to take home? I'll even make them specifically for you. Any type you want."

"You have a deal. I'll be expecting my donuts later this afternoon."

Cameron slid off the booth's bench seat. As Devin took his place, the werewolf snagged a chair from the table across from them and dragged it over to sit on.

Devin turned his head to look at the object of his desire. Kaisa had pushed herself into the corner so they didn't come in contact with each other. She stared across the table at her twin and his mate.

"Are you going to ignore me, Kaisa?"

She turned her gaze on him. "I will if you're only here to ask me out for the hundredth time."

"It hasn't been that many. You're exaggerating. It's more like fifty."

Kaisa rolled her beautiful green eyes. "And you think that's an acceptable number?"

"Of course. I'm hoping I'll wheedle you into saying yes before it gets to that point."

"And if that doesn't happen?"

"I guess I'll end up looking like a desperate loser, but I won't give up."

Rikki giggled. "Kaisa, you better put him out of his misery and go out with him."

Kaisa turned a scowl on her brother's mate. "That would only encourage him. Then he'd bug for a second date and then another, and another, and so on."

"Hello. I'm right here," Devin said. "And gee, don't make it sound as if going out with me would be such a bad thing." For the first time, he kind of lost it. The frustration of Kaisa turning him down time after time had finally gotten to him. "I realize you think I'm a player, but I've had no interest in another woman since I met you, Kaisa. You can believe that or not. It's true, though." In a quieter tone, he added, "And you not wanting to go out with me because I'm human, that's totally unfair, considering your brothers found their mates when they were humans."

Devin slid off the seat and then marched out the entrance. Maybe he should give up on Kaisa, but he really didn't want to. Deep inside, he knew she was the woman he wanted to have a solid, committed relationship with. It was too bad she wanted nothing to do with him.

He walked down the sidewalk with no real destination in mind, just needing to get away from Kaisa. He'd spend the rest of his break away from the coffee shop and then return by the back door so he wouldn't have to see her again.

About a block away from the shop, he was grabbed by the back of the neck and forced into the closest alley. He was turned as if he weighed nothing so his back landed against the brick wall of one of the buildings. He met Kaisa's pissed-off gaze.

"You don't get to make comments like that and then walk away," she said.

Devin went to push from the wall, but Kaisa put her hand on the center of his chest, effectively pinning him with no way to get free. She had three times the strength, even with the weight lifting he did.

"Yes, I do," he replied, his tone just as harsh as hers had been. "You don't think it ticked me off to hear what you said back there? Well, I have news for you. It did."

"I meant it as a joke."

He snorted. "Not entirely. Fine, you win. I'll stop asking you out. I now understand I'll never be good enough for you, the hybrid. You're special, and I'm just a dumb human. There are plenty of women I know who'd love to have a date with me and will have no problem getting really up close and personal. I'll give one a call right now."

Devin reached into his front jeans pocket and then took out his cell phone. Before he could do anything with it, Kaisa snatched it out of his hand.

"You're not calling one of the sluts you know," she said with a scowl.

"Why do you care?" he shot back. "As you've made it so painfully clear, I'm human. I don't have forever to live. I have to use the years I have. I'm no longer going to waste my time mooning over an immortal hybrid who doesn't have any feelings for me." He leveled a hard stare at her. "Give me my phone."

"No."

"Why? You don't like the idea of me seeing another woman? Too bad for you."

Kaisa let loose with an animalistic growl, took her hand off his chest to grab a fistful of his hair and slammed her mouth down onto his. Devin found himself unable to breathe as she kissed him so thoroughly his cock hardened to the point of pain in mere seconds. She claimed his lips with what felt like pent-up longing and lust.

Devin shoved his tongue into Kaisa's mouth and twined it with hers before running it along one of her fangs. Another growl rumbled out of her, which cranked his arousal even higher. He slid his hands down to her shapely butt and then angled her closer so he could grind his aching erection against her. He groaned as she pushed back.

That small sound had Kaisa stiffening. She jerked away

with hybrid speed so in a blink of an eye she stood with her back to the building on the other side of the alley across from him. He ran his gaze over her. Her green eyes glowed, which meant she was extremely turned-on like him. There was a sexy blush to her cheeks, and her chest rapidly rose and fell with her fast breathing. He'd thought her beautiful before, but like this, she was even more so. He wanted her back in his arms.

"Kaisa," he croaked as he reached toward her.

She ran off with her super speed to the opposite end of the alley and then disappeared around the corner. Devin closed his eyes and leaned his head against the brick wall that kept him upright. He took some deep breaths to force the arousal that continued to surge through him to cool. There was no way he could go back to the coffee shop with a raging hard-on.

He opened his eyes and gave a harsh chuckle as he realized Kaisa still had his phone. Devin bet she wouldn't be at the shop when he returned. Hopefully, she'd give Waverly or Brolach his cell before she left.

* * * *

Kaisa forced herself to walk at a normal speed for a human before someone saw her. She took the route that would be the long way to the coffee shop. She cursed herself for being an idiot as she fought to bring her body under control.

What was I thinking? The problem was she hadn't been. Kissing Devin was the worst possible thing she could have done. She'd only encouraged him when she needed the opposite to happen. Right?

Who was she kidding? That kiss had proved how good they actually were together. Even now Kaisa's pussy throbbed with unfulfilled desire. Devin's kiss had made her weak in the knees as she'd thought it would. She'd been fighting her attraction to him, but kissing him had blown that right out of the water. He'd had her craving more. A whole lot more.

She hadn't wanted a human male since...Kaisa stopped that thought before she could finish it. She wasn't going to think about *him*. Even though four hundred years had passed, she couldn't forget. It'd been a hard lesson for her to learn and had her turning to male werewolves whenever she could no longer ignore her body's need for sex.

Meeting Devin had made Kaisa want to break her own rule. He was laid back, funny, and very good-looking. He wasn't as tall as her brothers or Cameron, but Devin was tall enough at six feet to complement her five-feet-eight frame. He had the same light brown hair as his sister, which he kept short. His eyes were the same shade of hazel like Waverly's as well. And his body, it was muscular and defined in all the right places. Being pressed against him back at the alley, she hadn't missed how hard he was, especially in one area. Her pussy clenched at the remembered feel of his cock.

Not for the first time did Kaisa wish Cameron had ended up being her mate, and that she could think of him as more than a brother. It would have made her life so much easier. Neither of those things were possible, though.

Kaisa's steps slowed as she suddenly remembered what she held in her left hand. Devin's cell. Shit, she'd run off without returning it to him. She shouldn't have taken it in the first place, but the thought of him contacting another woman for a booty call had made her jealous, which in turn had pissed her off for feeling that way. That had then led to her kissing him when she'd let her emotions get the best of her.

She came to a standstill as she raised the phone so she could look at the blank screen. What she thought of doing next would invade Devin's privacy, but she really didn't care. Kaisa had to know how many women's numbers he had in his contacts or it'd drive her crazy.

With a swipe of her finger, she woke the cell. It didn't require a pass key to get into it. Kaisa hesitated for a few seconds before she hit the icon for the contacts list. Surprisingly, there weren't as many numbers as she'd expected. And none were females' names she didn't know. Devin had his family, Cameron, Torger, her, and a few male friends she'd heard him talk about listed. So he'd been bluffing when he'd said he'd call another female.

She hated the fact that that caused a weight to lift off her shoulders, feeling as if she could take a deep breath again. Kaisa wanted to fight it, but there was no point. It wasn't going to go away, like how she felt for Devin. The taste of him was still on her tongue, and she wouldn't forget it any time soon.

Kaisa finally arrived at the coffee shop. Torger, Rikki, and Cameron still sat at the booth where she'd left them. A quick scan of the room showed Devin wasn't anywhere to be seen. She spotted Waverly and waited for her to finish taking a customer's order before she approached.

She held out the cell to Waverly. "Can you give this back to Devin? It's his."

Waverly took it with a surprised expression. "Okay. He's in the kitchen if you want to do it yourself."

"No, I think it'd be better if you do it. I'm pretty sure he wouldn't want to see me right now."

"Are things all right between the two of you? If Devin did something to upset you, just tell me and I'll give him a smack upside the head."

"Don't do that. It wasn't him. I did it."

"Okay. For what it's worth, I think he really does care about you. I've never known him to be so into a woman before. I'll give him his phone."

"Thanks, Waverly."

Kaisa turned and walked toward the booth where the others sat. She'd tell them she was leaving, then head to the house she shared with Cameron. Torger had lived with them until recently. He'd moved into Rikki's apartment above the hardware store across the street from the coffee shop now that they were mated.

Cameron and Rikki nodded after Kaisa spoke to them all. Torger lifted a brow at her in question, but she shook her head to tell him she wasn't about to discuss her wanting to leave right then. He being her twin, she shared a connection with him. Both of them could easily pick up on the other's emotions.

After saying goodbye to Brolach, Kaisa left the shop and then went to the parking lot at the side of the building. She was glad she'd decided to drive herself there instead of taking Cameron up on the offer to go in his car with him.

Inside her car, and on the road toward home, Kaisa found her thoughts straying to how good it'd felt to kiss Devin. She pushed them aside. She was going to have to put some distance between them for a while until she got over what had happened. She'd stay away from the coffee shop for a few days and concentrate on trying to find the vampire who had to be hidden nearby.

The male was a cousin or uncle from Kaisa's mother's side of the family. And had managed to compel Rikki to try to kill Torger, not that the asshole knew that nothing would cause that to happen. That branch of relations hated the fact that she, Torger, and Brolach existed. To vampires, hybrids were an abomination. They thought one of their kind mating with a lowly werewolf was against the very rules of nature.

Four of her vamp family had hunted her mom and dad down in the new world and had killed them. They'd buried Brolach alive, and she and Torger had been "born" in the flames of the fire that had consumed their mother.

Now the vampires were back, hunting them. They'd managed to take out one of the four, and at least one of the other three was in the area. The asshole who had gotten to Rikki had gone to ground, and so far, none of them could find him. It was only a matter of time before he'd show up again and do something to strike against them.

CHAPTER TWO

Three days had passed since the kiss in the alley, and Devin hadn't seen Kaisa. She hadn't even come into the coffee shop with Cameron, Torger, and Rikki as was her usual want. Devin was starting to think she did her best to avoid him.

He'd subtly asked Torger and Cameron about Kaisa, if there was a reason she wasn't with them, but they'd just said she was busy hunting for the vampire. Devin got that it was something important, but he couldn't help feeling she used it as an excuse not to see him.

After his shift ended, Devin headed home with the intent of getting in a jog before he cooked his dinner. Even though he spent most of his day making donuts and helping with other food orders at the coffee shop, he enjoyed cooking for himself. He was good at it and hoped someday to be able to go to culinary school to get even better.

He arrived at his small bungalow that he rented and parked his car in the driveway. It didn't take Devin long to change into a pair of sweats and tank top. Before he left the house, he clipped his MP3 player to his waistband and then put the earbuds into his ears. With his favorite band's music playing, he set off at an easy jog.

The familiar rhythm of running settled over him, and he let his mind go to the place where it was just his music and the movement of his body. He called it getting into "the zone."

He'd reached the outskirts of town and was close to the local grain elevator. That was his usual spot to turn around to return home. He did a circle in the empty parking lot, then ran to the opposite side of the road, heading in the direction he'd come.

Devin had only run a few steps when something in some low-lying thick brush at the side of the road snagged his attention. He could just see a spot of pink through the branches. As he came closer, he slowed and then came to a stop. He peered closer, then sucked in a sharp breath. He ran toward what had caught his interest.

It wasn't just a piece of pink material as Devin had first thought. It was the shirt of the woman who lay there. As he pushed the brush aside, he cursed. There was no question that she was dead. Her eyes were sightless and fixed. There was also the fact her throat looked to have been torn into, as if something or someone had used their teeth to do it. The wound appeared to be exactly like the one Waverly had received when a vampire had almost killed her. This woman hadn't been as lucky as his sister to have a hybrid mate on hand to turn her and save her life.

Devin turned off his MP3 player before he pulled out his earbuds. He took his cell from his sweats pocket. If the dead woman's wound hadn't looked like it'd been done by a vampire, he would have called the police. Since that wasn't the case, he needed to let the ones who hunted the vamp know instead.

He walked to the graveled shoulder of the road. He thought of calling Torger or Brolach, even Cameron, but in the end decided to call Kaisa. It made more sense. She was the one who'd been on the hunt more than the others. And he hadn't settled on her to contact because he wanted to hear her voice and have the chance to see her. Maybe.

Kaisa answered after the fourth ring. "Devin."

"Hello to you too."

"Why are you calling me?"

"Don't worry. I didn't call to bring up what happened in the alley. I was out for a jog and found something. It's a dead woman with her throat torn out. The wound looks the same that Waverly had after that vampire finished with her. The body was dumped at the side of the road in some thick brush by the grain elevator."

"Shit. That means the vamp is definitely still here near town. I'll come out and meet you. I'm about a minute away."

"Okay. See you when you get here."

Devin ended the call, then put his cell phone into his pocket. He was thankful the grain elevator was closed for the day. His standing at the side of the road would have drawn some unwanted attention. Plus, he knew quite a few people who worked there. Working in the only coffee shop in town, he'd probably met most of the local townsfolk. And because of that, he was pretty sure the dead woman hadn't lived in Lemmon. He didn't recognize her.

It wasn't long before Devin spotted Kaisa's flashy, expensive sports car driving toward him. She pulled into the grain elevator's parking lot, got out of her vehicle and then hurried to him. Once she reached him, he pointed to the brush.

Kaisa went to the body and squatted beside it. She closely examined the dead woman's throat. She took hold of her chin and turned her head to the side before tugging down the collar of the woman's pink T-shirt.

"You're right," she said. Kaisa stood and came to stand

in front of him. "A vampire killed her. She also has some older bite marks that are scarred over. The bastard fed from her without healing her afterward. I don't remember seeing her around town. Do you?"

Devin shook his head. "No. I don't think she's from Lemmon."

"That's what I thought. Some vampires like to capture a human to feed from on a regular basis. They get off on causing fear in their victims. They keep the man or woman for a short time, then once they get bored with them, they drink them dry and dump the body. Our vamp must have brought her with him. I think he deliberately got rid of her now for us to find the body or to learn about it. It's his way of saying he hasn't gone anywhere, and that he figures he can do whatever the hell he wants and we can't stop him."

"Nice," Devin said sarcastically.

"I have to call the others and let them know. Torger and Cameron in particular will want to see the woman before we get rid of the body. It has the vampire's scent all over it."

"If his scent is on her, wouldn't that make him a dumbass? I would have thought he'd want to stay off your radar."

Kaisa snorted. "It wasn't something he forgot to get rid of. It's his conceit showing. He wants us to get his scent. He's daring us to find him. He thinks if we confront him, we'll lose."

"That still makes him a dumbass in my books. You already took out a vamp with your brothers and Cameron."

"He'd think it was blind luck on our part. Remember, vampires think werewolves, and especially humans, are beneath them. And hybrids are just plain abominations who don't deserve to live."

"Ahh," Devin said loudly. "Too bad they haven't figured out you, Brolach, and Torger can't ever be killed since you're true immortals. The vampires are way more vulnerable than any of you."

"Which gives us an advantage. I'm going to call Torger and Cameron now."

"What about Brolach?"

"I think it best we tell him after the fact. If Waverly finds out you're here, she'll want to tag along with Brolach. I think it best she doesn't see this. It might set off some bad memories."

Devin nodded. Kaisa was right. Waverly had nightmares every once in a while of being held captive by the vampire who'd tried to kill her. Seeing the dead woman wouldn't do her any favors.

He looked around the area as Kaisa made her phone calls. Devin settled his gaze on her, and greedily drank in the sight of her. He'd missed her these past three days. And he hadn't been able to get their kiss out of his thoughts. He'd awoken in the middle of the night a few times with a raging hard-on after dreaming of her, and their kiss going so much further.

Kaisa ended her last call and then pocketed her cell. She met his gaze. "Stop."

"Stop what?"

"Stop staring at me as if you want to eat me."

"Sorry. I can't help it. It's your fault. You kissed me first."

"Damn it. I'm not going to do this with you now. Torger and Cameron are on their way."

"All right. Then when?"

"Never."

Devin blew out a frustrated breath. "That's not going to happen. We have to talk about it. Since you've been avoiding me these last few days — and I'm sure you'll try to do the same thing after we're done here — we're going do it now while we're still alone."

"No."

MARISA CHENERY

"Yes, or I'll bring it up in front of your brother and Cameron. You know they'll back me up."

Kaisa snarled her upper lip, giving him a flash of her fangs in obvious irritation. "You would too, and so would they. Both of them know why there can be nothing between you and me. Still they think I should admit defeat and let you in."

Devin took a step closer. "Tell me then. Make me understand why you have this rule where you won't date or have a relationship with a human."

"I don't like to talk about it."

"Can't you at least reconsider it? Both your brothers found their mates in human women. Who's to say you won't be just as happy with me?"

"Brolach and Torger knew Waverly and Rikki were theirs right from the start. Their werewolf and vampire sides recognized them as their mates. There's no denying that once it happens. I'm female. I can't walk up to a male and know instantly that he's mine."

"You know what, babe? Humans haven't ever been able to do that, and we manage to fall in love and get married."

"Yeah, and that works out so well for your kind. Unlike you, there is no such thing as divorce in werewolves and vampires. That's because they mate for life and are truly happy."

Devin threw up his hands. "Can't you at least give us a try?" At the sound of two cars coming toward them, he quickly added, "I want one date. After the kiss in the alley, you owe me that, at least. Say yes or I'll tell Cameron and Torger what happened between us."

Kaisa narrowed her eyes. "Do you know how immature that makes you sound?"

"Yeah, but you forced me to it. They're almost here. What will it be?"

"Fine, you win. I'll go out with you. We'll discuss this later."

"That's all I wanted."

The cars pulled into the grain elevator's lot and parked on either side of Kaisa's vehicle. After Torger and Cameron climbed out of theirs, they joined them at the side of the road.

"Where's the body?" Torger asked.

Devin pointed in the direction of the brush. Cameron and Torger left Kaisa and Devin while they checked out the dead woman. They didn't take very long before they rejoined them.

"Now that we have the bastard's scent, we should hopefully have an easier time hunting him," Cameron said.

"Don't count on it," Torger replied. "He's toying with us."

Devin nodded. "That's what Kaisa basically said."

Torger blew out a breath. "Well, we can't leave the body here for others to find." He turned to Devin. "Cameron and I will take care of it. You head home. Where's your car?"

"I was out for a jog when I found her. I'll be getting home the same way."

"Kaisa will give you a ride."

She scowled at her brother. "I will?"

"Yes. I doubt the vampire has any servants around, but I'd feel better if Devin wasn't on the road right now."

Kaisa nodded. "All right." She turned and took a few steps across the road. Without looking back to see if he followed, she said, "Let's go, Devin."

He nodded at Torger and Cameron, then ran to catch up with Kaisa, who'd already reached the parking lot. At her car, he climbed into the passenger side as she slid into the driver's.

Since Kaisa had never been to his house, Devin had to give her directions. That was their only conversation until she pulled into his driveway and then put the car into park.

He undid his seatbelt and turned sideways to face her. "Is Saturday night okay with you?"

She set her gaze on him. "For what?"

"Our date. Don't tell me you forgot already."

"No, I just hoped you would."

"Not going to happen. I can pick you up at your place at around six."

"I'll drive myself."

"Then you can pick me up. We can eat and have a few drinks at R Bar."

"Why can't you meet me there?"

"If I did that, you'd leave as soon as we finished our meal. I'm not letting you off the hook that easily. This is going to be a real date where we spend part of the evening and night together."

Kaisa let loose with a wolf's growl. "Okay. I'll pick you up here at six thirty on Saturday. Don't make me wait for you."

"I'll be on time."

Devin quickly leaned in and kissed Kaisa's cheek before he got out of the car. He stood in the driveway as she backed onto the street. She didn't look his way or wave as she drove off.

He sighed and went to the front door. He had two days to figure out a way to win Kaisa over. One date wouldn't be enough for him. If only he knew what had happened to her to make her so dead set against being involved with a human. Asking Torger or Cameron was out of the question. They were too loyal to her to divulge something like that to Devin. He'd have to earn her trust enough to get her to talk about it. The problem was he had no idea how to do that.

CHAPTER THREE

It was Saturday, and Kaisa stood in her bedroom as she inspected herself in the mirror attached to her dresser. She picked up her brush and ran it through her hair. Satisfied, she put it down and then gave herself one final look over.

She didn't wear any makeup, and never had in her life. She didn't need it. And there was the fact she grew up as a member of a native tribe. The women wouldn't have touched the stuff, even if they'd known about it.

Kaisa hadn't dressed up for her date with Devin. They were only going to the R Bar. Plus, she was more comfortable in jeans and a T-shirt. She wore a black leather jacket since the nights were starting to get cooler now that summer was on the way out. The only thing different from her everyday wear was the high-heeled black suede ankle boots she'd changed into from her sneakers. She didn't get many opportunities to wear them, and a date qualified, even if it was just Devin she was going out with.

She left her room and stepped out into the hallway. Cameron was there, leaning against the wall beside her door. He pushed away from it and then followed her down the stairs to the main level.

"So, are you all ready for your hot date with Devin?" Cameron asked as he gave her a wink.

Kaisa cringed inside. She hadn't wanted Cameron or her brothers to learn about her date, but Devin had told them. She had a feeling he'd done it purposely so she wouldn't be able to back out at the last minute. He knew Cameron and Torger would make sure she didn't.

"It's not a hot date," she said irritably. "I only said yes because Devin made it so I couldn't turn him down."

"Yeah, that's right. I can't help wondering what he has on you. It has to be something good to make you finally cave in."

"That's none of your damn business."

Cameron chuckled. "Oh, it's definitely something good." He grew serious. "Give him a chance, Kaisa. Devin's a great guy. He isn't Thad."

She growled low in warning. "Don't ever say his name around me."

"Christ, Kaisa, it's time to get over that bastard. He's long dead and buried. You're alive. Don't let the ghost of him ruin the happiness you can have in your life. You've already let him have too much control over it as is."

"It might have happened four hundred years ago, but to me it still seems like yesterday."

"Only because you let it. I think of you as my sister, and I want you to be happy. You're the one preventing that from happening. If you don't like the idea that there's no real way to know if Devin is your mate, then turn him."

"No."

"Why not? That's what you offered Thad, and he turned you down."

"Cameron," she warned with a growl.

He ignored her. "In the end, it was best that he had. He wasn't meant for you. You just haven't been able to see

162

past that. Devin is different. The guy practically worships the ground you walk on. If I was able to turn him into a werewolf, I would have bitten him by now. I've seriously considered talking to Waverly about turning her brother. I know she'd do it. Maybe Brolach or Torger can be convinced to do it if she's unsure about it."

"Don't you dare." Surprisingly, the idea of her not being the one to turn Devin didn't sit well with her. There was always a bond that formed between a vampire, or hybrid, and the human they turned.

"Then don't push Devin away. If you come back here in an hour, or I call Devin at that time and you aren't with him, I'm going to march you right back to him."

Kaisa scowled. "What the fuck, Cameron. Since when did you feel you needed to get involved in my social life?"

"Since I've seen how happy Brolach and Torger are with their mates. It's time you found that as well. No more wallowing in self-pity."

She bared her fangs and hissed. "I'm done with this conversation. I'm leaving now."

Kaisa walked past Cameron to the front door. He and Devin had ganged up on her. She hated being manipulated, even if in some ways it was for her own good.

* * * *

Kaisa pulled into the driveway at Devin's house. There was no way she was going to his door and ring the bell. He wanted her to pick him up, and she was doing that. She laid on the car horn.

The door opened, and Devin stepped out. She couldn't stop herself from running her gaze over him as he walked toward her car. He wore a dark gray button-down shirt that was tucked into a pair of black jeans that hugged him, showcasing a trim waist and muscular thighs. She forced herself to quickly skim over his crotch. She was not going to check out his package, no matter how much she wanted to.

He slid into the passenger side. "See, I wasn't late. I was actually ready early."

She didn't respond to that as she backed onto the street. Silence reigned as she drove to the bar. It was on the awkward side, at least for her. She was decidedly underdressed compared to Devin. All she'd done was change her shoes for the date.

Once they arrived, she parked, and then they climbed out of the car. Devin came around to walk at her side. He captured her hand in his. She gave him a hard look.

"It's a date, Kaisa. Holding hands is part of it."

"Whatever."

She'd give him that one as a win. And it had nothing to do with the fact that having her fingers linked with his made her warm inside. No, nothing at all.

They walked into the bar and then found a table near the back. Once they sat, a waitress came and gave them a couple menus. She took their drink order. Kaisa asked for a beer the same as Devin had. Alcohol didn't affect her unless she drank a shit ton of it, which would give a human alcohol poisoning. Werewolves and vampires had a very high tolerance when it came to drinking.

"So, what do you want to eat?" Devin asked as he looked at his menu.

Kaisa scanned hers. "I think I'll have the steak, as rare as I can get it."

"I'm going to have the ribs."

The waitress returned with their drinks, then took their meal order before she left them alone once again.

Kaisa looked around. Being a Saturday, the place was fairly busy. There were quite a few people filling tables or seated on stools at the bar. Two guys sitting at a table waved in their direction, and Devin waved back.

"Friends of yours?" she asked.

"Yeah. Don't worry. They won't come over and try to talk to us since I'm with you, and they'll know we're on a date."

"Great," she said sarcastically. The town was small enough for everyone to almost know everyone. So it wouldn't be long before the news got around that Devin had been seen with her there.

Devin reached across the table and captured her hand. He rubbed his thumb back and forth across her knuckles. "Can you at least look as if you're enjoying yourself?"

"Why? Are you afraid it'll give you a bad rep as a lady's man?"

"No, but I'd feel better if you did seem to like being with me. Right now, I can't shake the impression that I'm putting you through torture or something. I didn't realize I was so terrible to be around."

Kaisa winced inside. She wasn't actually going out of her way to make the date enjoyable. She was being a bit of a bitch. If she wanted to get through this night and not completely ruin the friendship she had with Devin, she needed to tone it down. Trying to push him away with her bad behavior obviously wasn't going to work. It would only make things between them strained. Her older brother's mate was Devin's sister, after all. Waverly would feel uncomfortable if this date went terribly wrong and Devin could no longer stand the sight of Kaisa.

"Sorry," she said softly. "I didn't want to give you that impression."

"Let's have a few drinks and eat, then we'll take it from there. I don't want to make it so you hate me for this."

"I wouldn't do that. You know I have reasons for..." Kaisa let her words trail away.

"I know there's something. Maybe if you explained it, it'll help me understand."

She bit back the urge to snap her teeth at him. Having

Cameron bring up the subject of Thad earlier made it a sore point for her. It was as if she'd picked at a cut and it had bled again. She wouldn't take it out on Devin. She strictly held Cameron responsible for it.

"I'm not comfortable getting into it with you. Suffice it to say, I once was in a serious relationship with a human male and it ended badly. Really badly, to be honest."

"You can't let one bad experience make you paint all men with the same brush. I would never cheat on you, if that's what the jerk did. And you don't have to worry about me freaking out about what you are, since I already know you're a hybrid."

Devin had no idea how close to home he'd hit with that last comment. If only Thad had been cheating on her. She would have gotten over what he'd done to her a long time ago. Not even Torger or Cameron knew the full story of what had happened.

She was saved from saying anything else when the waitress arrived with their meals. Kaisa focused on her food. The steak was as rare as she'd asked for it, and it was really tasty. It was the first time she'd eaten at the bar. She, Torger and Cameron had come there for drinks before Torger had met Rikki, but they'd never ordered anything to eat. She'd have to tell Cameron how good the steak was since it was one of his favorite things to have.

Once their silence was on the verge of becoming uncomfortable, Devin saved Kaisa by starting a conversation about a prank he'd pulled on one of the other cooks at the coffee shop. Brolach had told her how Devin and his other coworkers were forever trying to one up each other on pranks, and how Trevor, Waverly and Devin's dad, was always giving them crap for it when he found out.

"Did your dad catch you this time?" Kaisa asked in between laughs.

Devin chuckled and shook his head. "Thank god, no.

He'd already left for the day, and since Paul and I were closing, we cleaned up the mess before dear old dad would see it. I'm sure he would have taken a strip off me if he had."

"One day you're going to go too far and he'll get really mad at you."

He waved her comment aside with a flick of his hand and a snort. "What's he going to do? Fire me?" Devin chuckled. "That won't happen. I have a share in the family business. I know for a fact he expects Waverly and I to take over the coffee shop once he's too old to work."

Kaisa took her bottom lip between her teeth. "You mean you will. Brolach and Waverly will have to move away before it gets to that point. Your parents will question why your sister isn't aging."

"We'll see."

The conversation moved on to other things. They finished their meals and then ordered a second round of drinks. Kaisa had to admit she enjoyed being around Devin when she wasn't trying so hard to push him away. He was funny and laid back, traits she liked in a male.

After they decided to leave, they left the bar and headed outside to her car. She drove them to Devin's place. According to the time, they'd only taken an hour and half at the bar. It was too early for Kaisa to go home or she'd have to face Cameron's displeasure.

She put the car into park and then turned off the engine. Without looking at Devin, she said, "Ah, I can't go home yet. Can I come inside?"

*

Devin looked at Kaisa. "Sure you can. Honestly, I thought you'd fight me on the idea. Why can't you go to your place?"

She gave him a look that said she wasn't too thrilled

with what she was about to say. "Cameron is the reason. He said if I didn't spend what he deems as enough time with you, he'd march me right back here. And he said he'd call to check to see if I was actually with you, and not just hanging around someplace else to make it look as if I was."

"Seriously?" he asked with a laugh.

"Yes."

As if on cue, Kaisa's cell rang. With an irritated look, she answered it. "Hello, Cameron…Yes, I'm still with Devin…You really don't believe me to the point you have to talk to him?…Fine. Hold on."

She held out her phone. "It's Cameron. He wants to talk to you. The dumbass."

Devin took the cell from her. "Hello, Cameron."

"So she still is with you," Cameron said on the other end.

"Yes. Kaisa has been a great date. We're going into my house, so I'm have to hang up now." Devin didn't wait for Cameron to say goodbye before he ended the call. He handed Kaisa her phone. "Did I get rid of him quick enough?"

She chuckled. "Yes. And I'm sure Cameron loved the fact you hung up on him."

With her sensitive hearing, Kaisa would have had no problem hearing both sides of the conversation. "Forget about him. Let's go inside."

They climbed out of the car. Devin walked ahead of Kaisa to the front door. He unlocked and then opened it before he stepped aside for her to enter ahead of him. After he was inside, he switched on the foyer light.

"It's not much, but it's home," he said.

Kaisa followed Devin into the living room. She looked around. "I have to say it's cleaner than I expected. Cameron is forever leaving his crap all over the place in our house. I reach a point where I get totally disgusted, gather up everything that's his and dump it onto his bed, usually when he's sleeping in it."

"I can't stand clutter. It drives me nuts." He gestured toward the couch. "Take a seat. Would you like another beer? I have some in the fridge."

"Sure." Kaisa sat on one end of the couch.

Devin quickly left her and went to the kitchen. He took beers out of the fridge, then twisted the caps off. He'd hoped to somehow convince Kaisa to come inside after they'd gone to the bar. He'd have to thank Cameron later for making it so pain free. Now alone with her, he was going to use it to his advantage. There was something between them, and he wouldn't let her deny it.

He returned to the living room and passed Kaisa a beer before he sat next to her. Devin reached for the TV remote and then turned on the television. He flipped through the channels until he found a movie.

They sat in silence, drinking their beers and watching television for a few minutes before Devin shifted closer so their thighs touched. Since she didn't move away, he oh, so casually put his arm around her shoulders. She stiffened but didn't do anything to get out of his embrace.

Being this close to her had his heart beating faster and arousal surging through him. God, he wanted her. Spending this time with her proved how much he enjoyed being around her. And how good they could be if they were together.

Devin played with Kaisa's hair as he took a sip of his beer. The lock he wrapped around his finger was soft and silky. He ached to have the long strands draped over his chest as she kissed it. His blood heated, and his cock hardened.

Kaisa turned her head to look at him. He met her gaze. "Devin, you have to stop."

"Stop what?"

"Whatever you're thinking. I can smell your arousal."

"I can't help what you do to me."

"That doesn't cha—"

Devin cut Kaisa off with his mouth on hers. He thoroughly kissed her, not holding back any of the pent-up need that had built inside him. He didn't let her deny him. He pushed his tongue past her lips and tasted her, giving each of her fangs a swipe.

She let out a defeated-sounding moan, then placed their beer bottles on the coffee table before she turned fully toward him. He did the same and wrapped her in his arms, tugging her closer. Her breasts flattened against his chest, her taut nipples scraping against him with each of her rapid breaths.

Their kiss deepened. Devin took hold of Kaisa's thighs and spread them apart before he yanked her hips toward him. She ended up on his lap with her long legs around his waist. Her jean-clad pussy landed on his cock. Even though their clothes were between them, it still felt damn good.

Kaisa pushed against him, and Devin fell back onto the couch. It wasn't wide enough for the two of them. He couldn't stop them from falling to the floor between it and the coffee table. He landed on his back with a grunt and her still on top him, her lips not once leaving his.

She ground against him as she growled, making him even harder. He moaned. He'd lost count of how many times he'd fantasized about having her in his arms just like that.

Kaisa left his mouth and kissed along the side of his jaw before she worked her way down the side of his neck. Devin turned his head toward his shoulder and groaned loudly as she dragged a fang across his skin. He lifted his hand and buried it in her hair at the back of her head to hold her there, wanting more than anything for her to bite him, to feed from him.

She nipped him and rode him faster. He lifted his hips

to match the pace she set. He panted, and just when he was at the point where he'd beg her to sink her fangs into him, she did.

Intense pleasure shot through Devin. With each pull of Kaisa's mouth, it was as if she set his body on fire. She continued to rock against him as she fed. It was the most erotic thing he'd ever experienced, and he wanted to be buried deep inside her pussy the next time they did this.

Just as he thought he couldn't take any more of the building pressure, he came, moaning, and feeling lightheaded. He closed his eyes. She cried out against his skin but didn't stop drawing at his neck. He drowned in the pleasure of it all.

*

Kaisa growled and moaned as her pussy clutched and released at nothing with her orgasm. Devin's rich blood continued to fill her mouth, and she greedily swallowed it down. The taste of him was like no other. She wanted more.

Once the last wave of her climax subsided, she realized Devin had gone completely limp, and how much of his blood she'd taken. She quickly pulled out her fangs, then dragged her tongue across his skin to seal and heal the wounds.

She sat up and looked down at him. His eyes were closed, and he was passed out. His heart beat steadily, but it seemed to work harder than it had. A skitter of unease ran down her back. She *had* taken too much.

Not once out of her entire long life had she ever fed so much that she'd put a human at risk. Her adoptive native parents had known exactly what she and Torger were and had taught them at an early age to only take what they needed from donors, to never lose control.

Kaisa didn't hesitate. She sank her fangs into the inside

of her wrist. Once the blood welled to the surface, she bent down, cupped the back of Devin's head and put her wrist against his mouth.

"Drink, Devin," she said as she gave him a little shake.

She breathed a silent sigh of relief once he closed his lips around her skin and took a deep pull. Her pussy clenched at the pleasurable sensation, but she pushed it aside. She'd fucked up. She'd let herself get too carried away.

After she figured he'd had enough, she tugged her arm away and sat up straight. Devin let out a sigh but didn't open his eyes. He'd slipped into a deep sleep.

Having what she'd done hit her, and hard, Kaisa quickly scrambled off Devin and stood. She had to get out of there. Now. Without looking back at him, she raced to the front door and then left. She drove away as if the hounds of hell snapped at her heels.

CHAPTER FOUR

Devin came awake and then let out a groan at the soreness in his back. He blinked open his eyes to find he lay on the floor between the coffee table and couch. He shifted and grimaced at the wetness inside the crotch of his jeans.

He jerked upright and looked around as everything came back to him in a rush. Damn, Kaisa wasn't there. She must have run after she'd fed from him, and he must have passed out afterward since he didn't remember her leaving. He wished she would have stuck around.

He looked at the clock on his cable box and had to do a double take. According to it, he'd been asleep for a couple hours, at least. No wonder his back was sore. He licked his lips and scowled at the coppery taste. It tasted like…

Devin shot to his feet and raced to the bathroom. He flipped on the light before he leaned closer to the mirror above the sink as he stared at his reflection. There was blood on his lips, and he was pretty damn sure it wasn't his. He turned his head to the side and looked at his neck where Kaisa had bitten him. There was no mark to show she had.

He looked directly into the mirror again, his gaze focused on his lips. Kaisa had given him her blood. It was the first exchange that put him onto the road to being turned. He didn't think she'd done it with that in mind. Devin would bet anything that she'd fed too deeply from him, which would explain why he'd passed out. Waverly and Brolach had done their first exchange for the very same reason. Brolach had lost control and had fixed it by giving Waverly his blood in return.

Devin grimaced again at the cool wetness in his jeans. He'd come all over himself. Nothing like embarrassing himself in front of Kaisa by acting like a virgin making out with his first girl.

He unbuttoned his shirt and then took it off before he peeled out of his sodden jeans. A shower was in order. And a load of laundry, which he'd do in the morning. After he turned on the water to the right temperature and then stepped into the tub, Devin couldn't help but smile.

Even though Kaisa would state tonight had ended in disaster, he didn't think it had. She no longer could push him away and say they weren't good together. She'd do her best to make sure the second blood exchange didn't happen, but he wasn't about to let her off the hook for that. He'd already settled his mind to the fact that the only woman he wanted was her.

* * * *

Kaisa drove through town and then ended up at the grain elevator. She parked in the lot and rested her forehead on the steering wheel as she mentally kicked herself for being an idiot. She should have never bitten Devin. It was the worst thing she could have done.

Now it was way too late. For both of them. She still had the taste of his blood in her mouth, and she wanted more.

More of it and the pleasure she'd found in his arms. She wanted him in the worst way. The attraction she had for him had increased to the point she couldn't just push it away. She'd thought she'd fallen for Thad hard and fast, but it didn't compare to what she felt for Devin. She was so screwed.

Kaisa lifted her head and straightened. She had no fucking idea what to do. All it would take to turn Devin was one more blood exchange. A small part of her said no way in hell would there be a second. A larger one wanted to rush back to his place and do it right there and then. And she knew damn well he'd be more than willing.

She put the car into drive and then headed back into town. She needed to talk to someone. The one person she always turned to in times like this was Torger. She and her twin would always have a close bond. He knew her better than anyone else, as she knew him.

Kaisa parked at the side of the road in front of Torger and Rikki's place. She stepped out of the car before she went to the door that led upstairs to their apartment. At the top, she knocked on their entrance door.

Rikki answered it with a smile, flashing her fangs. "Hey, Kaisa. We weren't expecting you. Come in."

She crossed the threshold. Rikki shut the door behind her. "It was a last-minute decision. Is it okay if I talk to Torger?"

"Of course. You don't need to ask. I was about to get into the shower." Rikki looked toward the open bedroom door. "Torger, Kaisa wants to talk to you."

Torger came into the living room as Rikki headed to the bathroom. Kaisa sat on the couch next to her brother once he took a seat. He turned sideways to face her.

"So, sis, what brings you here? I thought you had a hot date with Devin."

Kaisa cringed inside. Hers and Devin's date had definitely turned out to be hotter than she had expected. "I was out with him. That's why I need to talk to you."

Torger grinned. "What happened? You ended up having a better time than you thought?"

She blew out a breath. "You could say that."

"I knew you would. Now you can stop pushing him away and—"

"I fed from Devin, lost control, and took too much blood. I had to feed him some of mine so I made the first blood exchange," she hurriedly blurted.

Torger's smile fell and he blinked a few times, as if he hadn't quite understood what she'd said. "You made a blood exchange with Devin?"

"Yes. I didn't set out for it to happen. Things became…heated…between us after we went to his house. Kissing led to me biting him, and I ended up getting lost in the moment. It was either I give him my blood or a trip to the nearest hospital and try to explain why he'd need a transfusion."

He smiled again. "There's nothing wrong with that."

"Ah, yeah, there is. I can't be with him. He's human."

"Ah, yes, you can. And there is an easy remedy for that. Do the last blood exchange and he'll be a vampire."

"I can't."

"Why? I really don't understand. You obviously have feelings for him, which you managed to keep hidden until now."

"What makes you think I feel something for Devin?"

"Hello? You lost control while you fed from him. The first time I took Rikki's blood, it was like nothing I'd had before. I was addicted from that point on. You can't deny you feel the same way about Devin's."

"That happened to you because Rikki is your mate. Devin isn't mine."

"You don't know that. Turn him and you'll know for sure. He'll be able to sense it."

"No."

Torger ran his gaze over her face. "You're afraid to in case he does end up being your mate."

"No, I'm not. You know my history when it comes to a relationship with a human male."

"Don't compare Devin to that asshole, Thad. Devin would jump at the chance of being turned. So you got burned once. It's time to take another leap of faith for someone who could make you happy."

Exasperated that Torger would basically tell her the same thing Cameron had earlier, Kaisa shot back, "You don't know the full story of what happened between Thad and me at the end." She snapped her mouth shut once she realized what she'd just let out of the bag.

Torger scowled. "What are you talking about? You told me that Thad refused to be turned and no longer wanted to be with you anymore because of what you are."

It was too late to take back what she'd said now. "It was so much worse than that. Not only did he not want to be turned, he took the news of me being a hybrid really, really badly. After I showed him my wolf, he figured I was a witch. He set the church on me. I didn't see it coming. They tried to capture me to try me as a devil worshipper. I escaped, but not without killing a few of the church's men."

Her brother snarled and growled low in his throat. "Why the fuck didn't you tell me? I would have killed the bastard."

"I was stupid and still had feelings for Thad, even though he would have let them take me away and torture me. It took me years to get over him."

"If that shit wasn't already dead, I'd hunt him down and kill him."

"I know. Now you understand why I have trust issues when it comes to human men."

Torger took hold of her hand. "Yes, but don't let the bastard win. It's no longer the 1700s. Humans aren't as stupid and naïve now as they were back then. Devin knows exactly what you are and has no problem with it. If you don't give him a chance, you could be throwing away the best thing to happen to you."

Kaisa smirked. "You sound like Cameron. He gave me a speech along those lines before I left to pick up Devin."

He gave her a crooked grin. "Well, great minds think alike."

She rolled her eyes. "You mean ones that won't bloody well mind their own business, more like."

"We just want what's best for you." Torger glanced toward the bathroom as the shower shut off. "Seriously, though, I think you're letting what happened with Thad cloud your judgment when it comes to Devin. Do the second blood exchange. Plus, think about the fact that there is at least one vampire around here. Turning Devin will help protect him. He's going to be walking around town with the scent of your blood in his. Do you want him to be vulnerable to a vamp? He could almost be killed like what happened to Waverly or one could use compulsion on him to do something terrible same as happened to Rikki." He stood, then pulled Kaisa to her feet. "Now get out of here. I want to enjoy the rest of the night with my mate. Just the two of us."

Kaisa sighed. "Fine, I'll go. And I'll think about what you said."

"Good."

She let herself out of the apartment, then walked down the stairs to street level. Outside, Kaisa climbed into her car. Her one moment of weakness had not only put Devin on the road to being turned, but also made him an easy mark for a vampire if one stumbled across him. It seemed as if fate was going to force her to seriously come to a decision about how she felt for him and make her decide what to do about it.

* * * *

Late morning the following day, Devin's cell phone rang. He looked at the screen to see who it was and ended up having his mouthful of coffee go down the wrong way. He tried to cough up a lung to clear it before he answered.

"Hi, Kaisa," he croaked.

"What's wrong? Your voice sounds funny."

He coughed again. "Sorry. I was choking on some coffee." He cleared his throat. "There. All better now."

"Oh. Well, try not to drown yourself." She paused. "I think we should meet somewhere and discuss what…happened last night."

"I agree. You ran off on me."

"That isn't something I'm proud of. I got spooked."

"I know you were. You can come here if you want."

"All right. I'll be over in twenty minutes."

"Sounds good."

Devin ended the call and looked down at himself. He wore pajama bottoms and a T-shirt. And he hadn't even brushed his teeth yet that day.

After doing what he needed to do in the bathroom, he went to his bedroom and put on a clean pair of jeans and T-shirt. He brushed his hair and then put on some cologne. For some stupid reason, he now had a case of nerves about seeing Kaisa again. He'd been really surprised that she'd called. He'd figured he'd have to be the one to hunt her down and confront her about had happened between them.

Devin had a feeling his nervousness stemmed from the fact he wanted her even more than he had before. He didn't know if it was him just being silly, but he felt as if he already shared a connection with her because they'd made the first blood exchange.

He went to the living room and sat on the couch to wait for Kaisa's arrival. Devin had no idea what she'd say. He had strong feelings for her and wanted what Waverly had with Brolach, but he wasn't really sure how Kaisa felt about him. There was no denying that lust ran hot and heavy between them. That wouldn't be enough for a real relationship to take root, though.

Exactly twenty minutes after Kaisa had phoned, his doorbell rang. Devin stood and went to answer the door. He opened it and smiled. He stepped back for her to come inside. He closed the door behind her.

"Let's sit in the living room," he said.

She followed him into the room and then sat next to him on the couch. Kaisa's gaze strayed to the floor where they'd ended up last night. That brought it all back to the forefront of his mind. How good it'd felt to kiss her, have her fangs in his neck as she fed. It reminded him that he'd embarrassed himself by coming in his pants.

Devin cleared his throat. "So last night."

Kaisa met his gaze. "Yeah."

"Before you say anything else, I want to tell you I don't normally have a problem with…holding back. I don't have a premature problem with my equipment, if you know what I mean."

She gave him a small smile. "I know. When a female vampire feeds from a human male, especially the first time, that can happen. It's normal."

"So in other words, it was as if I lost my virginity all over again."

"I guess in a way, yeah," she said with a chuckle.

"Good to know. So the next time you feed from me, I shouldn't embarrass myself like that again."

Her face grew serious. "About me biting you last night, I have to apologize for my lack of control. I don't normally take so much blood. I put you at risk. That was the reason for me giving you my blood. It was either that or a trip to the nearest hospital for a transfusion, which would have caused questions we couldn't answer."

Devin reached across and took Kaisa's hand. "No need to apologize. I'm fine. Look, I'm going to be brutally honest with you. I want you to turn me. I want to be a vampire like Waverly."

"I'm not…ready to do that right now. I thought about this a lot last night. I think we should see each other more before taking that big step."

"What changed your mind?"

"Torger. After I ran from you, I went to talk to him. I can tell him anything, and he says what I need to hear, whether I think I do or not. He's always to the point with me." Kaisa blew out a breath. "I told you I had a bad experience with a human male, and it's left its mark. What I didn't say is that it happened four hundred years ago. To make a long story short, Thad didn't take what I was very well and set the church on me. He'd told them I was a witch and a devil worshipper. If I hadn't been a hybrid, I'm sure they would have captured me and tortured me before eventually killing me."

Devin let out a quiet curse. He brought her hand to his mouth and kissed her fingers. "You know I'd never do anything like that to you, right? That shit was done by people who were uneducated and very superstitious, especially about things they didn't understand. I have true feelings for you, Kaisa. We can make this work. And once you turn me, and I end up being your mate, it'll be even better."

"There's no guarantee you will be. What will you do once you're a vampire and I'm not yours?"

He tugged her toward him. "We won't think that way. That's not even a possibility for me. Now let's work on getting to know each other better. Very intimately. I haven't been able to stop thinking about last night."

Devin didn't give Kaisa a chance to deny him as he covered her lips with his. She didn't push him away. With her free hand, she fisted the front of his shirt and yanked him even closer as she hungrily kissed him back.

Remembering how this was how things had started the night before, Devin broke away from Kaisa, stood and pulled her to her feet with him. He bent and then picked her up over his shoulder. She let out a surprised cry as he turned and headed in the direction of his bedroom.

"What are you doing?" she asked with laughter in her voice.

"We're going to continue this in my room on my bed where we'll be more comfortable."

Inside his bedroom, he crossed to his king-sized bed. At the foot of it, he gently placed her onto the mattress. He climbed up with her and settled next to her before he took her mouth once more.

Devin slipped his tongue past her lips when she opened for him. He swept it across each of Kaisa's fangs, eliciting a moan from her. His cock hardened and throbbed. He'd waited months to get her into his bed, had ached for her. Now that she was there, he'd do everything he could to make her not want to leave it.

He dragged his hand down her side, following her curves before reaching up to settle a palm on one of her breasts. He squeezed it before he brushed his thumb back and forth across her taut nipple. She arched her back, pushing the mound closer.

Kaisa rolled toward him and thrust her hips along his, rubbing her jean-clad pussy against his straining erection. Devin took that as a sign that she wanted more. He was more than willing to oblige.

Devin pulled away before he lifted her shirt off over her head. He looked down at her breasts, which were encased in a satin and lace bra. He kissed the tops of them as he unhooked the garment. Kaisa tugged the straps down her arms, then threw it over the side of the bed. He slid down the mattress until he was eye level with her nipples. He took one into his mouth and sucked. She sank her fingers into his hair to hold him there.

"More, Devin," Kaisa said with a moan.

He nuzzled her other nipple. "I'll give you exactly what you need."

"Faster."

He pushed her onto her back and rose onto his bent arm as he worked on undoing her jeans. "I've waited too long for this to rush. I'm going to savor you."

Devin pushed her pants down past her hips, then pulled them from her legs and off. He ran his gaze over her almost-naked body. It was perfect and made him ache to be inside her.

He placed a kiss between her breasts before he continued downward. Once he reached the top of her panties, he hooked them with a finger. Her stomach quivered as he licked and kissed her there and removed her underwear. He sent the piece of satin and lace flying over his shoulder. He now had her exactly where he wanted her—naked in his bed and wanting him.

CHAPTERFIVE

Kaisa sucked in a sharp breath as Devin once more kissed her belly. Her pussy ached to have his cock buried deep inside it. And her fangs had dropped and throbbed in time with her rapidly beating heart. She was so turned-on, she was sure her werewolf side made her eyes glow.

Devin slowly worked his way lower on her body, kissing and licking as he went. He settled between her spread thighs, his broad shoulders opening them wider. Kaisa just about came off the mattress at the first swipe of his tongue along her pussy. She couldn't hold back a growl of need.

He laved her from bottom to top, circling his tongue around her clit. Her arousal ramped up even more. As he continued to pleasure her, she couldn't deny he was talented when it came to oral sex.

He thrust two fingers inside her as he sucked her clit. Devin worked the digits in and out, hitting the right spots to have her gasping. She lifted her hips to match his strokes.

Kaisa sank a hand into Devin's hair and tugged. "I don't want to come this way. I want you inside me when I do."

Devin pulled his fingers out of her as he gave her clit one last suck. He shifted up her body and then laid on his side next to her. "Then undress me, Kaisa." His voice was husky with arousal.

She didn't waste any time in pushing him to his back and then stripping his shirt and jeans off. His underwear quickly followed. His fully engorged cock stuck out straight from his body. A bead of pre-cum glistened on the tip.

She reached out and fisted his shaft, pumping up and down. He thrust into her palm with a groan. He was long, thick and hard. He'd feel so damn good inside her. As she stroked his erection, she couldn't stop her gaze from drifting to the side of his neck where the large artery rapidly pulsed. The thought of sinking her fangs into him as his cock speared in and out of her pussy made her even wetter.

Kaisa forced herself to look away from Devin's neck. She wasn't going to bite him. She could take too much of his blood again, and that wouldn't be good. She didn't want to turn him yet. Even if he did end up not being her mate, there would remain a bond between them since she'd be his sire. She wanted to make sure they could make things work before taking that final step.

With a tight rein on her need to bite him, Kaisa shifted to straddle his hips. She fisted his cock, then led it to her slick pussy. She took the tip inside before she gradually worked his entire length into her.

Devin reached up and palmed her breasts. "God, Kaisa. You feel even better than I imagined. Move on me."

She rose onto her knees, then sank onto him, impaling herself to the hilt once more. He was right. It did feel good. Really good. He stretched and filled her all the way up.

Kaisa rode him up and down, setting a faster pace. She angled her hips so his cock rubbed her in all the right places. An orgasm built deep inside her, and with it, her fangs throbbed even more. The urge to drink Devin's blood threatened to overwhelm her. Only with him did her control slip.

She growled as he thrust his hips up to meet her downward strokes. They panted, straining for that ultimate pleasure. Kaisa's climax took her by surprise. It tore through her and wouldn't be held off. Her pussy clutched and released Devin's cock as it stroked in and out. She moaned, riding out the waves of her orgasm.

Once it ended, Devin took hold of her hips to keep their bodies joined as he rolled them so she was on her back. He took her mouth in a heated kiss as he thrust into her at a fast pace. She tightened her inner walls around his length. He moaned as he came. His erection pulsed deep inside her pussy.

Devin collapsed on top her, then switched positions with her. She lay sprawled along him as she fought to catch her breath. The urge to bite him diminished now that she'd climaxed. She relished the afterglow as he stroked his hands up and down her back.

"If you tell me you didn't enjoy that, I think I'll spank you," Devin said.

Kaisa chuckled. "I can't very well say that when you gave me a screaming orgasm." She lifted her head off his chest to look at him. "I don't think we'll be leaving your bed much today."

He cupped her face and kissed her. He smiled as he pulled away. "I won't argue with that. Just don't wear me out too much. I do have to get up early tomorrow to work. People, especially Cameron, will be upset with you if I don't get my baking done for the coffee shop."

"I promise. I don't need Cameron bitching at me because he has to go through donut withdrawal. He'd go wolf and bite my ass."

"Speaking of wolf. Why don't you show me yours? I've been dying to stroke all that fur. Then you can take on your human form and I'll stroke you even more."

Kaisa reached for her wolf side and shifted to her animal form. Devin could pet her all day if he wanted. Her wolf eyes just about rolled to the back of her head as he did just that.

* * * *

Kaisa came awake, not sure what had awoken her. She lay on her side, close to the edge of the bed. She turned her head to find Devin asleep. He was on his back, stretched out to take up more than half the king-sized mattress. He quietly snored. She rolled to her other side with a smile. The man was a bed hog. She'd have to have a little chat with him about that in the morning. If she slept over, she wanted to be comfortable.

She realized in which direction her thoughts had headed. Kaisa had already planned to sleep over at Devin's house a lot. It was after the third time they'd made love that she'd made the decision. He was an unselfish lover, and the way he touched her, he made her feel cared for. It'd been too long since she'd let a man into her life, other than to scratch an itch.

Devin didn't know it yet, but he'd won her over. He'd done a thorough job of taking away all her memories of sleeping with Thad and replacing them with better ones. She could now say she'd put her first love behind her. No more would she let him and what he'd done to her have any bearing over her life. Devin would give her the fresh start she hadn't known she so badly needed.

Kaisa closed her eyes to try to go back to sleep. It was at least three hours before dawn, and Devin would be getting up early. Her eyes snapped open at a sound of something or someone moving around near the back entrance to the house. That was what must have awakened her.

She quietly slipped out of the bed. Devin slept on. He wouldn't have heard the sounds coming from outside. They weren't loud enough for a human's range of hearing. Kaisa gathered up her clothes from the floor and then hurriedly dressed. She wasn't going to investigate the noise naked.

Walking silently, she left the bedroom and then headed to the back entrance. It was a regular wood door in the kitchen that led to the backyard. It had a window in the center with a curtain covering it. She pushed the material to the side and peered out. There was a man on the patio, pacing back and forth. She didn't recognize him, and the way he stumbled every once in a while, it was obvious he had a hard time seeing in the dark, which meant he wasn't a vampire.

Not sure why he was there or what he wanted, Kaisa unlocked the door to step outside. Now that she'd decided to let Devin into her life, it was her responsibility to watch over him until she turned him. As a human, he was vulnerable. And having a strange human male at his back door in the middle of the night made her extremely uncomfortable.

She silently slipped out the door and then closed it behind her. "Why are you here?" she softly asked as she closed some of the distance between her and the man.

He didn't acknowledge that he saw her or even heard her. He kept pacing the patio, seemingly lost in his own world.

"Hey. I asked you a question." She grabbed him by the arm and pulled him to a stop.

He jerked his head in her direction. "It worked."

She scowled. He didn't react like a normal person would. "What?"

Three male vampires rushed her before she even sensed

they were there. Kaisa tried to fight them, but there were too many of them. She growled in frustration as they subdued her.

One smacked her across the face. "You'll stop that animalistic sound. We don't need to be reminded of your disgusting hybrid heritage."

Kaisa bared her fangs and hissed. That earned her a punch to the jaw. Stunned from the blow, the three easily bound her hands behind her back with heavy chain she'd have no chance of breaking. They did the same to her ankles. Lastly, they gagged her.

The human male quietly laughed as one of the vampires picked her up and slung her over his shoulder. As she was carried away, the human once more took up his pacing.

* * * *

Devin's alarm went off, dragging him from a deep sleep. He turned onto his side and reached over to the bedside table where the digital clock sat. Without opening his eyes, he silenced the annoying noise. Seven o'clock in the morning seemed too early, especially since he'd been up way later than he'd normally be on a Sunday night.

He smiled as he remembered the reason for staying up past his bedtime. Devin rolled to his back and turned his head to the spot next to him. His smile drifted away at the empty side of the bed.

He sat up. "Kaisa?" he called. There was no reply. He listened to see if he could hear her moving around, thinking she could have gone to use the bathroom. Nothing. "Kaisa?" he called again more loudly.

Damn. Had she run off again while he'd slept? Considering how the night had gone, he'd figured she was done with that. She'd said she'd stay until the morning.

Devin slid out of bed and then tugged on some pajama

bottoms. He left the bedroom and then went to the living room. He pulled back the curtain to look outside. He scowled as his gaze landed on Kaisa's car, which was still parked in the driveway. Where was she?

"Kaisa?" he called as he headed to the kitchen.

She wasn't there, but the first thing Devin noticed was that the deadbolt on the back door was unlocked. He always kept it locked unless he planned to sit on the patio or use the barbeque out there.

Devin crossed to the door and opened it. He stepped onto the patio and stopped short when he noticed the man pacing it. A quick search of the backyard showed Kaisa wasn't there either. What the hell was going on?

He went and stepped into the path of the stranger. "Who are you and what are you doing on my property?"

The man came to a sudden halt and gave Devin a smile that made him look a little crazy. "I have a message for you."

"From whom?"

"My master."

The man seemed to pull a knife from out of nowhere and lunged at Devin. He quickly caught the man's wrist before the blade could come in contact with the left side of his chest. With his free hand, he balled it into a fist and slammed it into the man's face. The stranger staggered but didn't stop the pressure he held on the knife.

Devin hit him again. The man was shorter and not very muscular, but that didn't stop him from doing his damnedest to push the knife home. Devin punched him in the head again and again. After the fifth hit, the man finally went down.

He kicked the knife out of his hand, then stared down at the unconscious stranger. His presence there and Kaisa's disappearance couldn't be a coincidence. Considering the man had used the word "master," it had Devin strongly believing a vampire was behind the two occurrences.

A sense of panic rose within him, but Devin pushed it back. Kaisa was a hybrid. She was a true immortal. Nothing could kill her, but she could still feel pain. If a vampire did have her, there was no telling what he would do to her.

Devin dragged the man into the kitchen by his heels, not caring that his head banged against the ground. Once inside, he grabbed two zip ties that he had in his junk drawer. He rolled the man onto his stomach, then tied his hands behind his back and his ankles together.

His captive secured, Devin rushed to the bedroom to get his cell phone. He called Torger, hoping like hell he'd pick up, even though it was so early in the morning. After the sixth ring Torger answered.

"Hello?" he asked groggily.

"Torger, it's Devin. Kaisa is missing."

"What? How would you know she's missing? Did Cameron call you?"

"No, he didn't. Kaisa spent the night at my place. I woke up, and she was gone."

"About time you two hooked up. Maybe she just got up before you and went home."

"No. Her car is parked in my driveway. She's nowhere inside or outside the house. I looked. Plus, there's the fact a man I've never seen before was in my backyard. He pulled a knife on me, saying he had a message for me from his master. He tried to stab me in the heart. I knocked him out and now have him tied up in my kitchen."

"Don't go anywhere," Torger said. "I'll call Brolach and Cameron. We'll be there as soon as we can. What's your address?"

"Okay. Just hurry up. I have no idea when Kaisa went missing. My alarm woke me up, and she was already gone." He quickly gave Torger his address.

Devin ended the call, then hurried to get dressed. He pulled on the first pair of jeans and T-shirt he touched. He returned to the kitchen. The man was still out cold. He went to the front door to unlock it for the others' arrival.

While he waited, Devin paced to the kitchen to keep his eye on his captive, then to the living room to look out the window to see if Torger, Brolach, and Cameron had arrived. As the minutes ticked by, his nerves stretched taut. He could only imagine what Kaisa could be going through right this very minute. He hated that he couldn't do anything to help her. He'd never be any match to a vampire, not as a human. He ceased pacing as two cars came to a hurried stop on the street in front of his house.

Devin opened the front door as the three men ran up to it. He waved them inside. "I have the man in the kitchen."

They all went to the room where Devin's captive lay. Torger squatted beside the man and sniffed. He looked at Brolach and Cameron, who then did the same.

"He's definitely a servant to a vampire. I can't tell which one, though. He has the scent of three of them on him," Torger said.

Brolach nodded. "I recognize them. I'll never forget their scents. They're the three vamps who killed our parents." He snarled his upper lip and growled. "Now that all of them are in the area, we're going to end this."

Torger straightened, along with Cameron and Brolach, and looked at Devin. "Show us where you found the servant."

Devin led them out through the back door to the patio. "He was here, pacing."

Cameron did a circle of the patio. "I can slightly pick up Kaisa's scent. It's been hours since she was out here. Same with the three vamps. The human servant's and Devin's scents are the strongest."

Brolach let out a growl as he walked toward the back of the property. "They took her." He stopped at the fence. "I lose the scent trail here. It's too old."

"Well, let's wake up the servant. He might have been

compelled to not give away the location where the vampires are holed up, but there's a chance the assholes are so sure of themselves they didn't bother," Torger said as he turned to head back to the house.

Inside the kitchen, the servant was still unconscious. Devin crossed to the sink, took out a glass, filled it with cold water, then threw the liquid onto the servant. He came awake, sputtering.

Brolach grabbed the servant by the back of his shirt and hauled him to his feet. He turned the man to face him. "Where is your master, and where did they take my sister?"

The man laughed. "My master is here, there, and everywhere." He laughed again, sounding a bit maniacal.

"Ah, I don't think he's all there in the head, if you catch my meaning," Devin said.

Torger sighed. "That happens sometimes when the master vampire compels his or her servant too many times. I have a feeling this one hasn't been compelled to keep the vamps' location a secret. I doubt he'll be much use to us. That's why he was left behind to try to take out Devin. They must know he and Kaisa are close."

Devin grabbed the servant from Brolach and gave the man a hard shake. "Tell us where Kaisa is."

"I have a message from my master."

He shook him again. "You already tried that and failed."

The servant looked at Brolach and Torger. "This message is for them. The twin and older brother. My master said you are to meet him and his cousins tonight at midnight by the grain elevator."

Devin shook him for a third time. "That's it?"

"That's all my master said."

He let the man go. "I guess that's all we'll get. What are we going to do with him now?"

"Lock him up somewhere," Cameron said. "Once his

master is dead, he'll no longer be a servant. I don't want to kill him for something he had no control over."

"I agree," Torger said with a nod. "Cameron, you'll be responsible for him when Brolach and I go the grain elevator tonight."

"I'm going with you," Devin cut in.

Brolach shook his head. "No, you aren't. Waverly would be extremely mad at me if something happened to you. I don't want her to get a dog house and put me in it in the backyard."

Cameron snorted. "Dude, she wouldn't physically put you in a dog house. It's a figure of speech to mean you'd be on her bad side."

Brolach was still learning modern-day sayings, and took them literally, which ended up being funny. Devin wasn't in the mood for laughing right then, though.

"I'm going with you," he firmly stated.

Torger sighed. "Devin, you're human. You wouldn't last two seconds up against a vampire, especially ones as old as these."

Devin leveled his gaze at Torger. "Then turn me. Make me a day walker. Kaisa and I have already done the first blood exchange. You can do the second. It's what I want. I've fallen for your sister. I don't care if we're not mates, but I want the chance to have forever with her. Turn me."

Torger looked at Brolach. "What do you think?"

"Do it. I have a feeling he'll follow us no matter what we do or say to dissuade him. He's strong as a human, but he'll be even stronger as a vampire. Plus, there's the fact the vamps won't be expecting him to be turned. It might give us an advantage. And I'm going to say that it seems right that you do the second blood exchange with Devin since you're Kaisa's twin."

"All right. I'll turn you. Hopefully, Kaisa won't try to take my head off once we get her back. You and I will have a bond afterward. Not like a mate bond, but there will be a connection since I'll be your sire."

"I'm okay with that. Let's do this." Devin turned his head to the side so Torger would have better access to his neck.

Torger chuckled. "Sorry, but I'm not biting you on the neck. That's for more intimate feedings. I'll bite the inside of your wrist. That's where you'll drink from me. Just be prepared for it not to feel like it did when you did this with Kaisa. You're going to feel it."

Before Devin could say anything, Torger took hold of his right wrist, turned it over and sank his fangs into it. Devin suck in a sharp breath. That fucking hurt. Torger took two long pulls before he swiped his tongue along Devin's skin to heal the wound. Torger bit into his wrist, then offered it to Devin. He didn't hesitate to take it and sucked two mouthfuls down. He released him. Torger licked the bite mark, which disappeared.

At first, Devin thought nothing happened until a sensation built inside him. It bordered on the edge of pain. His breathing quickened as he looked at the others.

"It's okay," Torger said. "The sensation doesn't last long."

Devin nodded as it grew and his upper gums and eyeteeth felt as if they were on fire. As promised, the very uncomfortable feeling slowly receded. A quick test with his tongue showed he now had fangs. His senses had increased exponentially. He could pick up the individual scents in the room, could tell the difference between human, werewolf, hybrid, and vampire. His eyesight was sharper, keener. And his hearing was strong enough he heard insects moving in the grass in the backyard. It seemed to bombard him all at once.

Torger smiled. "Welcome to the family. You'll quickly adjust to your new senses. It took Rikki about an hour. It should be the same for you."

"How are you feeling?" Brolach asked.

Devin took a deep breath. "Good. Like really good. I feel stronger, as if I could move mountains."

"Excellent. We have until midnight to teach you how to fight like a vampire. I suggest we call Waverly so she can tell your dad we won't be in to work today. She always knows what to say to him."

"Crap," Cameron said. "No new donuts today."

Devin shook his head. "I think we'll be a little busy to worry about that. Plus, there will be some. My dad will make them. He's the one who taught me."

As Torger helped Brolach make a call to Waverly on his cell phone, Cameron took charge of the servant and forced him to sit at the kitchen table. Devin squeezed his hand into a fist. He was stronger. He couldn't wait to test out his new vampire strength.

CHAPTER SIX

Kaisa came awake in a closed, dark space that was moving. It didn't take her long to figure out she'd been stuffed into a trunk of a car. A stake was through her heart. It didn't leave her immobile as it would vampires, but it left her weak.

The three vamps had brought Kaisa to their den straight from Devin's place. It was located outside town at a farm. They'd claimed the large basement of the house as theirs. As they'd carried her through, the owners had seemed to look right through them as if they weren't there. She'd tried to get their attention. One of the vampires had laughed and had seemed to take great relish in telling her the entire family had been compelled to think nothing out of the ordinary happened around them, that their home hadn't been taken over by vamps. Nor would they be able to see or hear what went on around their unwanted guests.

Kaisa had spent the day locked in the darkness of the basement with the three vampires and four of their servants. The vamps had slept while the servants guarded her.

She'd tried to take on her wolf form and escape the chains that bound her but had quickly found out that avenue of getting free had been taken from her. As she'd tried, the metal in the links had heated to a glowing red and had burned her skin. A servant had laughed, saying his master would be pleased to hear the witch's spell had worked. That the spelled chains would keep her from shifting.

So there she was, staked and chained, unable to do anything to free herself. She had no idea what the vampires had in store for her. It wasn't as if they could kill her. The only thing that had worried her was what they could possibly do to Devin. Her vampire relatives had to know she and Devin had become close, had to have had her watched, and seen where she'd been over the course of the week.

If anything happened to Devin, she'd never forgive herself. As she sat in that basement for hours with nothing to do but think, Kaisa came to terms with the fact she'd gone and fallen in love with another human male. She could finally admit that he'd started to claim a piece of her heart from the very first day they'd met.

The car came to a stop. Kaisa pushed thoughts of Devin aside, needing her full attention on what would happen next. The trunk opened, and one of the vamps roughly pulled her out of it. She looked around as two of them grabbed her by an arm and dragged her away. She instantly recognized where they were. They were parked at the side of the road near the grain elevator, close to the spot where Devin had found the body of the dead woman.

They dragged her toward the parking lot of the elevator where Torger's car sat. He and Brolach climbed out and then came to stand in the middle of the large, open space. The vamps came to a stop a few yards in front of her brothers.

"Let Kaisa go," Brolach said with a growl.

The vampire who didn't hold her stepped forward. "No. You two will give yourselves to us. Your kind should never have been allowed to exist. We will rectify that."

Torger shook his head and laughed with no humor. "You're an arrogant bastard, aren't you? Didn't you learn two thousand years ago that we can't be killed? You tried to end Brolach's life, yet here he is. You burned our mother's body, yet Kaisa and I were born in her ashes. The reason you dislike hybrids so much is the fact we're stronger than you. We're true immortals. You aren't."

If Torger had wanted to goad them into going on the attack, he'd said the right things to make it happen. Two of the vamps launched themselves at Brolach and Torger. The third only hissed, but kept a firm hold on Kaisa. Staked and chained, there wasn't a damn thing she could do to help her brothers.

As they met and struck out against the two vampires, she growled, hating the feeling of being helpless. So focused on the fight, Kaisa almost lost her balance as the vamp who held her was torn from her side. She looked around to find Devin had a hold of him from behind, the vampire's head wrenched back. Devin opened his mouth, flashing a set of fangs he hadn't had that morning.

He easily held the struggling vampire. "I'll get you free of those chains once I take care of this piece of garbage."

Devin sank his fangs into the vamp's neck and tore out his throat. Blood sprayed. He drank it, then once he had his fill, he ripped the vampire's head clean off his body before tossing it away.

Kaisa could only stare at Devin. He was a vampire. And god, he was hottest thing she'd ever seen. He'd been strong before, but now that he'd been turned, his muscles looked even more pronounced.

He crossed to her and easily broke the locks to her chains. As the links fell to the ground, he ripped out the stake in her chest. Kaisa sucked in a sharp breath at the sudden pain and stumbled. Devin caught her and held her close.

"You okay?" he asked as he kissed the top of her head.

"Yes." She pulled back to look at him. "Who?"

"Torger. They figured it was better he do it since he's your twin. We can talk about this later. Let's help your brothers clean up the rest of the trash."

Brolach and Torger had no problem standing up to the two remaining vampires, but with Kaisa's and Devin's help, the vamps didn't have a chance of winning. They soon lost their heads as the other had.

They all stood with the dead at their feet, panting. Kaisa had a hard time taking her gaze off Devin. There was something definitely feral about him now. Something that Waverly and Rikki hadn't gotten after the second blood exchange. Nor had Kaisa's female friend, the human she'd turned many years ago. Devin was the first male to become a day walker. Maybe that had something to do with it.

Torger ran his gaze over Devin. "Shit, man. You've turned out to be bloodthirsty. I didn't know you had it in you."

Devin put his arm around Kaisa's shoulders and pulled her up against his side. "They took what is mine. Kaisa is mine to protect. No one tries to hurt her and lives."

Kaisa sucked in a breath at Devin's words. Was he...? Brolach spoke before she could say anything.

"Ah, Devin," her older brother said. "Do you have this almost overwhelming urge to protect Kaisa? That she's yours and that you don't know if you could survive without her?"

Devin seemed to think for a few seconds, then nodded. "It's exactly like that. As soon as I saw Kaisa with those vamps, it took everything in me to stay hidden as we'd planned and not rush to her."

Torger looked at Kaisa. "Well, sis, you got what you

wanted. Your human-turned-vampire recognizes you as his mate."

"Is that true?" Devin asked as he turned his gaze on her.

Kaisa smiled. "Yes. That's what a male vampire feels once he meets his mate. And god forbid anyone gets in his way."

Devin wrapped her in his embrace. "I need to be alone with you. Now."

Torger chuckled. "I'll drive you to Devin's place since Cameron is at home with the servant, who will no longer be one." He looked at Brolach. "You going to be okay starting to clean up this mess until I get back?"

Brolach nodded. "Of course. Take them home."

* * * *

Kaisa stood with Devin at the front door of his place and watched Torger drive away. Once he disappeared from sight, she turned to her mate. She still wanted to pinch herself over the fact that he truly was hers. The months that she'd tried to push him away since he'd been human had all been a waste of time she could have had with him. If only she'd listened to him in the beginning and turned him.

She met Devin's gaze. "I'm sorry."

He smiled. "For what?"

"For trying to keep you at arm's length. I let a past relationship that happened so very long ago almost come between us. I knew you wanted to be turned. I should have done it, taken the gamble that you could have been my mate. Now it turns out you are."

Devin rested his forehead against hers. "That doesn't matter. It worked out in the end." He picked her up. "I'm going to clean up, then we'll make this mate thing official."

She had no problem with that. He unlocked the door

before he carried her inside. He didn't stop walking until he reached his bedroom. He placed her on the bed, then stripped out of his clothes. He was already fully aroused. She licked her lips.

Devin groaned. "This is when I'm very thankful for vampire speed."

He darted away, the shower ran for a few seconds, then he was back. The blood on his face was gone, and his hair was damp from being washed. He smelled like the soap he'd used.

Devin would have climbed onto the bed with her, but Kaisa held up her hand to stop him and went to stand in front of him. "Let me check out this new body of yours."

"Take your clothes off first," he said huskily.

Kaisa quickly complied. Once she was naked, she ran her fingertips down his chest. "I had no idea you'd be this strong once you were turned."

"It was a nice surprise. I felt strong after Torger turned me, but over a period of an hour, I kind of got muscles on top of muscles. Your brothers think because I'm male, and that I had two blood exchanges with two hybrids, might be the reason, which is just a guess."

"I'm not complaining. It just means I have to learn your body all over again."

Kaisa went on tiptoes and kissed Devin. Her fangs dropped, and so did his. They scraped against her lips, which caused her to shudder in pleasure. Once they were breathing heavily, she dragged her fangs along his neck and down to his chest. He moaned.

She continued downward until she ended up on her knees in front of his hard cock. Her pussy throbbed as arousal surged through her. She licked the moisture that leaked from his slit before she carefully took him inside her mouth. She sucked him almost to the back of her throat. He moaned louder.

She took his cock in and out until he pulled on her arm

to stand. Kaisa was more than ready to take him inside her body. She ached for him. She ached to have him sink his fangs into her along with his shaft.

Kaisa thought Devin would put her on the bed, but he had other plans. He lifted her and placed her legs around his waist as he braced his feet on the floor. He reached between them, fisted his cock, then led it to her slick opening. With a thrust of his hips, he buried his length inside her pussy.

In a show of strength, he held her by the bottom and lifted her on and off his cock. All she could do was hold on to his shoulders. He continued to slide in and out of her as he buried his face in the crook of her neck. Kaisa turned her head to the side, knowing exactly what he wanted.

"Do it," she said on a moan. "Bite me. Make me yours. I love you, Devin."

He groaned. "God, I love you too. I can't hold back any longer. I have to taste you."

She threaded her fingers into his hair to hold him to her. He sank his fangs into her as her body coiled tighter, an orgasm building deep inside her. As he drank, it tore through her, stealing her breath.

Once it was over, Devin licked her skin to heal his bite. He continued to spear in and out of her as she sank her fangs into his neck. He bellowed with pleasure, and his cock pulsed deep inside her pussy.

Devin carried her to the bed and slowly laid her down, keeping their bodies joined. They were now mated. The bond had formed between them. He was now forever hers. And to think, if she'd had her way, she would have missed out on the best thing to ever happen to her. The vamps who'd killed her parents were no longer a threat. Kaisa could now enjoy life to the fullest with her mate.

The End

ABOUT THE AUTHOR

Marisa Chenery was always a lover of books, but after reading her first historical romance novel she found herself hooked. Having inherited a love for the written word, she soon started writing her own novels.

She now writes young adult books and erotic romances.

Marisa lives in Ontario, Canada, with her boyfriend, Steve, her four children, four grandchildren (she's a young grandma in her fifties), and rabbit and dog.

www.marisachenery.com

www.ingramcontent.com/pod-product-compliance
Lightning Source LLC
Chambersburg PA
CBHW020953180626
46814CB00003B/1071